A Novel by Vonda N McIntyre

Star Trek
The Wrath of Khan

Screenplay by Jack B Sowards
Based on a story by Harve Bennett
and Jack B Sowards

Futura
Macdonald & Co
London & Sydney

A Futura Book

First published in Great Britain in 1982
by Futura Publications, a Division of
Macdonald & Co (Publishers) Ltd
London & Sydney

ISBN 0 7088 8095 9

Reproduced, printed and bound in Great Britain by
Hazell Watson & Viney Ltd, Aylesbury, Bucks

Futura Publications
A Division of
Macdonald & Co (Publishers) Ltd
Maxwell House
74 Worship Street
London EC2A 2EN

Paramount Pictures Presents
STAR TREK®:
THE WRATH OF KHAN

Starring

WILLIAM SHATNER   LEONARD NIMOY
DeFOREST KELLEY

Co-Starring

JAMES DOOHAN   WALTER KOENIG
GEORGE TAKEI   NICHELLE NICHOLS

Also Starring

BIBI BESCH

and

PAUL WINFIELD as Terrell

Introducing **KIRSTIE ALLEY** as Saavik

and Starring **RICARDO MONTALBAN** as Khan

Music Composed by **JAMES HORNER**

Executive Consultant **GENE RODDENBERRY**

Based on **STAR TREK**

created by **GENE RODDENBERRY**

Executive Producer **HARVE BENNETT**

Screenplay by **JACK B. SOWARDS**

Story by **HARVE BENNETT**

and **JACK B. SOWARDS**

Produced by **ROBERT SALLIN**

Directed by **NICHOLAS MEYER**

A Paramount Picture

STAR TREK®:
THE WRATH OF KHAN

For Jane and Ole,
with love and snarks

Prologue

Captain's Log: Stardate 8130.5

Starship *Enterprise* on training mission to Gamma Hydra. Sector 14, coordinates 22/87/4. Approaching Neutral Zone, all systems functioning.

Mr. Spock, in his old place at the science officer's station, gazed around at the familiar bridge of the *Enterprise*. The trainees, one per station and each under the direction of an experienced crew member, were so far comporting themselves well.

It was a good group, and the most able of them was the young officer in the captain's seat. Spock expected considerable accomplishments from Saavik. She was young for her rank, and she enhanced her natural aptitude with an apparently inexhaustable capacity for hard work.

Spock listened with approval to the cool narration of the captain's log. Saavik, in command of the *Enterprise*, completed the report and filed it. If she were nervous—and he knew she must be—she concealed her feelings well. Her first command was a test; but even more, every moment of her life was a test. Few people could understand that better than Mr. Spock, for they were similar in many ways. Like Spock, Saavik was half Vulcan. But while Spock's other parent was a human being, Saavik's had been Romulan.

Mr. Sulu and Ensign Croy had the helm.

"Sector fourteen to sector fifteen," the ensign said. "Transition: mark." He was a moment behind-time, but the information was not critical to their progress.

"Thank you, Helm Officer," Saavik said. "Set us a course along the perimeter of the Neutral Zone, if you please."

"Aye, Captain."

Sulu watched without comment, letting Croy do his own work and make his own mistakes. The data streamed past on Spock's console.

Spock had not failed to notice Saavik's progress in the use of conventional social pleasantries. Trivial as they may have seemed, learning to use them was one of the most difficult tasks Spock had ever tried to master. Even now, he too frequently neglected them; they were so illogical, but they were important to humans. They made dealing with humans easier.

Spock doubted that Saavik would ever use the phrases with warmth, any more than he would, but she had modified her original icy disinterest, which had come dangerously close to contempt.

Saavik gazed calmly at the viewscreen. She was aesthetically elegant in the spare, understated, esoterically powerful manner of a Japanese brush-painting.

"Captain," Uhura said suddenly, "I'm receiving a signal on the distress channel. It's very faint. . . ."

Saavik touched controls. "Communications now has priority on computer access for signal enhancement."

Uhura's trainee worked quickly for several seconds.

"It's definitely an emergency call, Captain."

"Patch it through to the speakers."

Communications complied.

"Mayday, mayday. *Kobayashi Maru,* twelve parsecs out of Altair VI . . ." The voice broke up into static. The trainee frowned and stabbed at the controls on the communications console.

Spock listened carefully. Even computer-enhanced, the message was only intermittantly comprehensible.

". . . gravitic mine, lost all power. Environmental controls . . ."

"Gravitic mine!" Saavik said.

". . . hull broached, many casualties." The signal-to-noise ratio decreased until the message slid over into incomprehensibility.

"This is U.S.S. *Enterprise*," Uhura's trainee said. "Your message is breaking up. Give your coordinates. Repeat: Give your coordinates. Do you copy?"

"Copy, *Enterprise*. Sector ten . . ."

"The Neutral Zone," Saavik said.

Mr. Sulu immediately turned his attention from the speakers to his console.

"Mayday, *Enterprise*, we're losing our air, can you help? Sector ten—" The forced calm of the voice began to shatter.

"We copy, *Kobayashi Maru*—" The communications trainee and Uhura both glanced at Saavik, waiting for instructions.

"Tactical data, *Kobayashi Maru*. Helm, what does a long-range sensor scan show?"

Sulu glanced at Croy, who was understandably confused by the screen display. It had deteriorated into the sort of mess that only someone with long experience could make any sense of at all. Sulu replied to the question himself.

"Very little, Captain. High concentrations of interstellar dust and gases. Ionization causing sensor interference. A blip that might be a ship . . . or might not."

The viewscreen shivered. The image reformed into the surrealistic bulk of a huge transport ship. The picture dissected itself into a set of schematics, one deck at a time.

"*Kobayashi Maru*, third class neutronic fuel carrier, crew of eighty-one, three hundred passengers."

"Damn," Saavik said softly. "Helm?"

Sulu glanced at the trainee, who was still bent over the computer, in the midst of a set of calculations. Croy shook his head quickly.

"Course plotted, Captain," Mr. Sulu said, entering his own calculations into the display.

Spock noted with approval Saavik's understanding of the support level she could expect from each of her subordinates.

Sulu continued. "Into the Neutral Zone." His voice contained a subtle warning.

"I am aware of that," she said.

Sulu nodded. "Entering Neutral Zone: mark."

"Full shields, Mr. Sulu. Sensors on close-range, high-resolution."

Spock raised one eyebrow. Gravitic mines were seldom deployed singly, that was true, but restricting the sensors to such a limited range was a command decision that easily could backfire. On the other hand, long-range scanners were close to useless in a cloud of ionized interstellar gas. He concentrated on the sensor screens.

"Warning," the computer announced, blanking out the distress call. "We have entered the Neutral Zone. Warning. Entry by Starfleet vessels prohibited. Warning—"

"Communications Officer, I believe that the mayday should have priority on the speakers," Saavik said.

"Yes, Captain." Uhura's trainee changed the settings.

"Warning. Treaty of Stardate—" The computer's voice stopped abruptly. The static returned, pierced erratically by an emergency beacon's faint and ghostly hoot.

"Security duty room," Saavik said. "Security officers to main transporter."

"Aye, Captain," Security Commander Arrunja replied.

"You may have to board the disabled vessel, Mr. Arrunja," Saavik said. "They're losing atmosphere and life-support systems."

"The field suits are checked out, Captain."

The intern accompanying McCoy on the bridge hurried to open a hailing frequency.

"Bridge to sick bay," she said. "Dr. Chapel, we need a medical team in main transporter, stat. Rescue mission to disabled ship. Field suits and probably extra oxygen."

McCoy looked pleased by his intern's quick action.

"One minute to visual contact. Two minutes to intercept."

"Viewscreen full forward."

The schematics of the ore carrier dissolved, reforming into a starfield dense and brilliant enough to obscure the pallid gleam of any ship. Ionization created interference patterns across the image.

"Stand by, transporter room. Mr. Arrunja, we have very little information on the disabled vessel. Prepare to assist survivors. But—" Saavik paused to emphasize her final order, "—no one is to board *Kobayashi Maru* unarmed."

"Aye, Captain."

"Coordinate with the helm to open the shields at energize."

"Aye aye."

Spock detected a faint reflection at the outer limits of the sensor sphere. The quiet cry of the distress beacon ceased abruptly, leaving only the whisper of interstellar energy fields.

"Captain, total signal degradation from *Kobayashi Maru*."

"Sensors indicate three Klingon cruisers," Spock said without expression. "Bearing eighty-seven degrees, minus twelve degrees. Closing fast."

He could sense the instant increase in tension among the young crew members.

Saavik snapped around with one quick, frowning glance, but recovered her composure immediately. "All hands, battle stations." The Klaxon alarm began to howl. "Visual: spherical coordinates: plus eighty-seven degrees, minus twelve degrees. Extend sensor range. Mr. Croy, is there a disabled ship, or is there not?"

The viewscreen centered on the ominous, probing shapes of three Klingon cruisers.

"I can't tell, Captain. The Klingon ships are deliberately fouling our sensors."

"Communications?"

"Nothing from the Klingons, Captain, and our transmission frequencies are being jammed."

"Klingons on attack course, point seven-five c," Spock said.

Saavik barely hesitated. "Warp six," she said.

"You can't just abandon *Kobayashi Maru!*" Dr. McCoy exclaimed.

"Four additional Klingon cruisers at zero, zero," Spock said. Dead ahead. Warp six on this course would run the *Enterprise* straight into a barrage of photon torpedoes.

"Cancel warp six, Mr. Croy. Evasion action, zero and minus ninety. Warp at zero radial acceleration. Visual at zero, zero. Dr. McCoy," Saavik said without looking back at him, *"Enterprise* cannot outmaneuver seven Klingon cruisers. It will, however, outrun them. If we lure them far enough at their top speed, we can double back even faster—"

"And rescue the survivors before the Klingons can catch up to us again," McCoy said. "Hmm."

"It is the choice between a small chance for the disabled ship, and no chance at all," Saavik said. "If there is in fact a disabled ship. I am not quite prepared to decide that there is not."

The viewscreen confirmed four more Klingon ships dead ahead, and then the *Enterprise* swung away so hard the acceleration affected the bridge even through the synthetic gravity.

"Mr. Sulu, Mr. Croy, lock on photon torpedoes. Fire . . ." She paused, and Spock wondered whether her early experience—fight or be killed—could, under stress, win out over regulations and the Federation's stated object of keeping the peace. "Fire only if we are fired upon."

"Aye, Captain." Sulu glanced at the young ensign beside him. Croy clenched his hands around the firing controls. "Easy," Sulu said quietly. The ensign started, then forcibly relaxed his hands.

Another blip on the sensor screens: "Enemy cruisers, dead ahead." A third group of ships arrowed toward them, opposing their new course.

Saavik said something softly in a language with which Spock was not intimately familiar, but by her tone it was a curse.

The Klingons fired on the *Enterprise*.

"Fire at will!" Saavik said.

The viewscreen flared to painful brightness before the radiation sensors reacted to the enemy attack and dimmed the screen to half-intensity. The energy impact was so severe even the shields could not absorb it. Spock held himself steady against the wrenching blow, but it flung Sulu from his post. He crashed into the deck and lay still. McCoy and the intern vaulted down the stairs to the lower bridge and knelt beside him.

"Mr. Sulu!" McCoy said. His tricorder gave no reaction. "Spock, he's dead."

Spock did not respond.

"Engineering!" Saavik said.

"Main energizer hit, Captain," Chief Engineer Scott replied.

Saavik slammed her hand down on her controls, transferring command to the helm. She took Sulu's place. Croy fought for data enough to aim the torpedoes.

Saavik did the calculations in her head, keyed them into the console, transferred a copy to Croy's station, and spoke to Scott in the engine room.

"Engage auxiliary power, Mr. Scott. Prepare to return fire . . . *now*." She fired. One of the Klingon cruisers fired on the *Enterprise* just as Saavik's torpedo hit. The cruiser imploded, collapsing in upon itself, then exploded in eerie, complete silence. But its death-blow struck the *Enterprise* full force. The screen blazed again, then darkened, with the radiation of the furious attack.

"We're losing auxiliary power, Captain, and our shields along wi' it," Scott cried. "The ship canna take another—"

The scream of irradiated electronics cut off Scott's warning. The enemy ships in pursuit caught up to the Starfleet vessel. At close range, they fired. The *Enterprise* shuddered, flinging Uhura against the railing and to the deck. McCoy left Sulu's inert body and knelt beside the communications officer.

"Uhura—Uhura . . . Oh, my God," McCoy whispered.

Saavik fired at the Klingons, but nothing happened.

"Mr. Scott, all power to the weapons systems; it's our only chance."

"Mr. Scott . . . is a casualty. . . ." his assistant replied. Her voice was drowned out by a flood of damage reports and pleas for medical help. "Environmental controls destroyed." "Life support, nonfunctional." "Gravity generators failing."

McCoy cursed at the intraship communications. "Dr. Chapel, I've got to have a team on the bridge! Dr. Chapel! Chris!"

But he got no reply at all from sick bay.

Saavik touched the photon torpedo arming control one last time, delicately, deliberately, yet with the realization that nothing would happen.

"There is no power in the weapons systems, Captain," Spock said. He felt the gravity sliding away. "There is, in fact, no power at all; we are merely bleeding the storage cells."

The enemy ships enclosed them, hovering at the vertices of an impenetrable polyhedron. Spock saw the final attack in the last fitful glow of the viewscreen.

Firing their phasers simultaneously, the cruisers enveloped the *Enterprise* in a sphere of pure energy. Spock imagined he felt the radiation flaming through the ship. He grabbed for a handhold.

His console exploded in his face.

As he fell, he heard the wailing hiss of escaping air, a sound that had been the last experience of all too many spacefarers.

Saavik, clutching at the helm officer's console, fighting the ship's quakes, turned just in time to see Mr. Spock fall. For an instant, she wished only to be ten years old again, so she could scream with fury and the need for revenge. Dr. McCoy struggled toward Spock, but never made it; the convulsions of the ship flung him down. He screamed, and collapsed with a groan.

Saavik stood up. Her ship, her first command, lay dead in space; her crew was destroyed by her incompetence. She opened the hailing frequencies, not even knowing whether any communications were left at all.

"Prepare the escape pods," she said. "All hands, abandon ship." She armed the log buoy and fired it out into space. It would testify to her failure, yet also to her honor in accepting the responsibility.

"All hands," she said again. "Abandon ship."

Chapter 1

Sitting in front of the viewscreen, Admiral James T. Kirk shook his head. He laughed softly, but more at memories than at what he had observed.

"All right," he said. "Open it up."

The wall in front of the video console parted and opened, revealing the destroyed bridge of the *Enterprise*. Kirk got up and walked into it. Acrid smoke burned his eyes, but the heavy-duty ventilation system had already begun to clear the air. He stepped carefully through shattered bits of equipment, over Dr. McCoy's body, and stopped in front of Lieutenant Saavik. She met his gaze without flinching.

"May I request the benefit of your experience, Admiral?"

"Well, Lieutenant, my experience is that the Klingons never take prisoners."

Saavik's expression hardened. Kirk turned all the way around, surveying the wreckage.

This could have happened to me, he thought. It almost did, all too often and not in simulation, either.

"Okay, folks," he said. "The fun's over." He glanced at the upper level of the bridge. "Captain Spock?"

Spock got smoothly to his feet. A scattering of breakaway glass shivered to the floor and crunched beneath his boots.

"Trainees to debriefing," he said.

The young crew members, still stunned by the realism of the test, got up and moved toward the exit. The more experienced bridge crew rose from being dead or injured, laughing and joking.

Uhura got up and brushed bits of scorched insulation from her uniform. Sulu turned over and sat up slowly.

"Was that rougher than usual, or am I just getting old?" he said. He climbed to his feet.

Dr. McCoy lounged on the deck, lying on his side with his head propped on his hand.

Kirk stood over him. "Physician, heal thyself."

McCoy gave him a hurt look. "Is that all you've got to say?"

"I'm a Starfleet officer, not a drama critic," Kirk replied.

"Hmph."

"It's too bad you're not a cook," Mr. Sulu said to the admiral.

"A cook? Why a cook?"

"You could make fried ham," Sulu said, deadpan.

Jim Kirk started to laugh.

"Fried ham?" Dr. McCoy exclaimed. "I'll have you know I was the best Prince Charming in second grade!"

"And as a side dish," Sulu said in the tones of an obsequious waiter, "perhaps a little sautéed scenery? When it's cooked it's much easier to chew." In an uncanny imitation of Dr. McCoy, he cried, "Mr. Sulu! Mr. Sulu! Oh, gods, Spock, he's dead!"

McCoy glanced at the ceiling in supplication, but then he could not stand it any longer. He began to laugh, too. From the upper bridge, Spock watched them, his arms folded.

McCoy wiped tears from his eyes. "Mr. Sulu, you exaggerate."

"Poetic license," Sulu said.

"Speaking of poetic license, or dramatic realism, or whatever," McCoy said, serious for a moment, "you hit the floor pretty hard. Are you all right?"

"I am, yes, but did they reprogram that simulation? I

don't remember its knocking us around quite so badly before killing us."

"We added a few frills," Kirk said. "For effect." He turned toward Saavik, who had watched their interplay as dispassionately as Spock. "Well, Lieutenant, are you going down with the sinking ship?"

He had the feeling she had to draw herself from deep thought before she replied. She did not answer his question; but then his question had after all been purely rhetorical.

"The simulation is extremely effective," Saavik said.

"It's meant to be." Kirk noticed, though, that she appeared as self-possessed and collected now as when she had entered the simulator, unlike most of the other trainees, who came out sweating and unkempt.

"But I question its realism."

"You think it's an effective simulation, *and* you think it's unrealistic?" Kirk asked.

"Yes, sir." Her imperturbability was not as complete as she pretended; Kirk could see the anger building up. "In your experience, how often have the Klingons sent ten cruisers after a single Starfleet vessel?"

"Lieutenant," Kirk said with an edge in his voice, "are you implying that the training simulation is unfair?"

She took a deep breath and did not flinch from his gaze. "Yes, I should have been more direct. I do not think the simulation is a fair test of command capabilities."

"Why?"

"The circumstances allow no possibility of success."

Jim Kirk smiled. "Lieutenant Saavik, do you think no one who worked on the simulation, and no one who ever took it before, ever noticed that the odds couldn't be beaten?"

She started to reply, stopped, and frowned. "No, Admiral," she said slowly. "I admit I had not considered that possibility."

"You were given a no-win situation. That's something any commander may have to face at any time."

She looked away. "I had not considered that, either." She made the admission only with difficulty.

"By now you know pretty well how you deal with life, Lieutenant. But how you deal with death is important, too, wouldn't you agree?"

"I—" She cut herself off as if she would not trust herself to answer.

"Think about it, Lieutenant," Kirk said. "Just think about it. Carry on." He turned to leave. At the top of the stairs, he came face-to-face with Dr. McCoy. "What's the matter with *you?*"

"You don't think you could manage to push just a little bit harder, do you?" McCoy said softly.

Kirk scowled. "They've got to learn, Doctor. We can't keep the reins forever. Galloping around the cosmos is a game for the young."

He crunched through the debris on the floor and disappeared down the corridor.

Sounding miffed, Uhura said, "What was *that* supposed to mean?"

McCoy shrugged, and shook his head. He and Commander Uhura left together.

Saavik sat alone in the ruins of her first command. She knew she must go to debriefing immediately . . . but she had many things to consider.

Jim Kirk trudged toward the debriefing room. He felt tired, and depressed: and oppressed, by the shining self-confidence of the young people he had been observing. Or perhaps it was by the circumstances of fate that made him the instrument for shaking and scarring that self-confidence. But McCoy was right: he *had* been too hard on Lieutenant Saavik.

He turned the corner and came face-to-face with Spock, who was leaning against the wall with his arms folded.

"Didn't you die?" Kirk asked.

He thought for an instant that Spock was going to smile. But Spock recovered himself in time.

"Do you want to know your cadets' efficiency rating —or are you just loitering?"

"Vulcans are not renowned for their ability to loiter," Spock said.

"Or for their ability to admit terrible character flaws, such as that they're curious."

"Indeed, Admiral? If it will raise your opinion of my character, I suppose I must admit to some curiosity."

"I haven't even got to the debriefing room yet, and you want an opinion." He started down the corridor again, and Spock strode along beside him.

"I seem to recall a Starfleet admiral who referred to this particular set of debriefings as 'a damned waste of time,'" Spock said. "He had a very strong belief that actions were more important than words."

"Did he?" Kirk said. "I don't believe I know him. Sounds like a hothead to me."

"Yes," Spock said slowly. "Yes, at times he was known as a hothead."

Kirk winced at Spock's use of the past tense. "Spock, those trainees of yours destroyed the simulator and you along with it."

"Complete havoc is the usual result when *Kobayashi Maru* comes upon the scene." He paused, glanced at Kirk, and continued. "You yourself took the test three times."

"No!" Kirk said with mock horror. "Did I?"

"Indeed. And with a resolution that was, to put it politely, unique."

"It was unique when I did it," Kirk said. "But I think a number of people have tried it since."

"Without success, you should add. It was a solution that would not have occurred to a Vulcan."

Jim Kirk suddenly felt sick of talking over old times. He changed the subject abruptly. "Speaking of Vulcans, your protégée's first-rate. A little emotional, maybe—"

"You must consider her heritage, Jim—and, more important, her background. She is quite naturally somewhat more volatile than—than I, for instance."

Kirk could not help laughing. "I'm sorry, Spock. The lieutenant is remarkably self-possessed for someone of her age and experience. I was trying to make a joke. It was pretty feeble, I'll admit it, but that seems to be about all I'm up to these days." He sighed. "You know, her tactic might even have worked if we hadn't added the extra Klingon attack group." He stopped at the debriefing room. "Well."

Spock reached out as Kirk started to go in. He stopped before his hand touched Jim Kirk's shoulder, but the gesture was enough. Kirk glanced back.

"Something oppresses you," Spock said.

Kirk felt moved by Spock's concern.

"Something . . ." he said. He wanted to talk to Spock, to someone. But he did not know how to begin. And he had the debriefing to conduct. No, this was not the time. He turned away and went into the debriefing room.

All those kids.

They waited for Admiral Kirk in silence, anxious yet eager. Lieutenant Saavik arrived a moment after Kirk sat down; Spock, his usual emotionless self once more, came in quietly and sat at the very back of the room. Jim Kirk was tempted to declare the discussion over before it had begun, but regulations required a debriefing; he had to fill out a report afterward—

That's all I ever pay attention to anymore, he thought. Regulations and paperwork.

He opened the meeting. He had been through it all a hundred times. The usual protocol was to discuss with each student, in reverse order of seniority, what they would have done had they been in command of the ship. Today was no different, and Kirk had heard all the answers before. One would have stuck to regulations and remained outside the Neutral Zone. Another would have sent in a shuttle for reconnaissance.

Kirk stifled a yawn.

"Lieutenant Saavik," he said finally, "have you anything to add? Second thoughts?"

"No, sir."

"Nothing at all?"

"Were I confronted with the same events, I would react in the same manner. The details might be different. I see no point to increasing your boredom with trivia."

Kirk felt embarrassed to have shown his disinterest so clearly. He reacted rather harshly. "You'd do the same thing, despite knowing it would mean the destruction of your ship and crew?"

"I would know that it *might* mean the destruction of my ship and crew, Admiral. If I could not prove that *Kobayashi Maru* were an illusion, I would answer its distress call."

"Lieutenant, are you familiar with Rickoverian paradoxes?"

"No, sir, I am not."

"Let me tell you the prototype. You are on a ship—a sailing ship, an oceangoing vessel. It sinks. You find yourself in a life raft with one other person. The life raft is damaged. It might support one person, but not two. How would you go about persuading the other person to let you have the raft?"

"I would not," she said.

"No? Why?"

"For one thing, sir, I am an excellent swimmer."

One of the other students giggled. The sound broke off sharply when a classmate elbowed him in the ribs.

"The water," Kirk said with some asperity, "is crowded with extremely carnivorous sharks."

"Sharks, Admiral?"

"Terran," Spock said from the back of the room. "Order Selachii."

"Right," Kirk said. "And they are very, very hungry."

"My answer is the same."

"Oh, really? You're a highly educated Starfleet officer. Suppose the other person was completely illiterate, had no family, spent most of the time getting thrown in jail, and never held any job a low-level robot couldn't do. Then what?"

"I would neither request nor attempt to order or persuade any civilian to sacrifice their life for mine."

"But a lot of resources are invested in your training. Don't you think you owe it to society to preserve yourself so you can carry out your responsibilities?"

Her high-arched eyebrows drew together. "Is this what you believe, Admiral?"

"I'm not being rated, Lieutenant. You are. I've asked you a serious question, and you've replied with what could be considered appalling false modesty."

Saavik stood up angrily. "You ask me if I should not preserve myself so I can carry out my responsibilities. Then *I* ask *you*, what are my responsibilities? By the criteria you have named, my responsibilities are to preserve myself so I can carry out my responsibilities! This is a circular and self-justifying argument. It is immoral in the extreme! A just society—and if I am not mistaken, the Federation considers itself to be just— employs a military for one reason alone: to protect its civilians. If we decide to judge that some civilians are 'worth' protecting, and some are not, if we decide we are too important to be risked, then we destroy our own purpose. We cease to be the servants of our society. We become its tyrants!"

She was leaning forward with her fingers clenched around the back of a chair in the next row.

"You feel strongly about this, don't you, Lieutenant?"

She straightened up, and her fair skin colored to a nearly Vulcan hue.

"That is my opinion on the subject, sir."

Kirk smiled for the first time during the meeting: this was the first time he had felt thoroughly pleased in far too long.

"And you make an elegant defense of your opinion, too, Lieutenant. I don't believe I've ever heard that problem quite so effectively turned turtle."

She frowned again, weighing the ambiguous statement. Then, clearly, she decided to take it as a compliment. "Thank you, sir." She sat down again.

Kirk settled back in his chair and addressed the whole class. "This is the last of the simulation exams. If the office is as efficient as usual, your grades won't be posted till tomorrow. But I think it's only fair to let you know . . . none of you has any reason to worry. Dismissed."

After a moment of silence, the whole bunch of them leaped to their feet and, in an outburst of talk and laughter, they all rushed out the door.

"My God," Jim Kirk said under his breath. "They're like a tide."

All, that is, except Saavik. Aloof and alone, she stood up and strode away.

Spock watched his class go.

"You're right, Spock," Kirk said. "She is more volatile than a Vulcan."

"She has reason to be. Under the circumstances, she showed admirable restraint."

The one thing Spock did not expect of Lieutenant Saavik was self-control as complete as his own. He believed that only a vanishingly small difference existed between humans and Romulans when it came to the ability to indulge in emotional outbursts. But Spock had had the benefit of growing up among Vulcans. He had learned self-control early. Saavik had spent the first ten years of her life fighting to survive in the most brutal underclass of a Romulan colony world.

"Don't tell me you're angry that I needled her so hard," Kirk said.

Spock merely arched one eyebrow.

"No, of course you're not angry," Kirk said. "What a silly question."

"Are you familiar with Lieutenant Saavik's background, Admiral?" He wondered how Kirk had come to pose her the particular problem that he had. He could hardly have made a more significant choice, whether it was deliberate or random. The colony world Saavik had lived on was declared a failure; the Romulan military, which was indistinguishable from the Romulan government, made the decision to abandon it. They carried out the evacuation as well. They rescued everyone.

Everyone, that is, except the elderly, the crippled, the disturbed . . . and a small band of half-caste children whose very existence they denied.

The official Romulan position was that Vulcans and Romulans could not interbreed without technological intervention. Therefore, the abandoned children could not exist. That was a political judgment which, like so many political judgments, had nothing to do with reality.

The reality was that the evolution of Romulans and Vulcans had diverged only a few thousand years before the present. The genetic differences were utterly trivial. But a few thousand years of cultural divergence formed a chasm that appeared unbridgeable.

"She's half Vulcan and half Romulan," Kirk said. "Is there more I should know?"

"No, that is sufficient. My question was an idle one, nothing more." Kirk had shaken her, but she had recovered well. Spock saw no point in telling Kirk things which Saavik herself seldom discussed, even with Spock. If she chose to put her past aside completely, he must respect her decision. She had declined her right to an antigen-scan, which would have identified her Vulcan parent. This was a highly honorable action, but it meant that she had no family, that in fact she did not even know which of her parents was Vulcan and which Romulan.

No Vulcan family had offered to claim her.

Under the circumstances, Spock could only admire the competent and self-controlled person Saavik had created out of the half-starved and violent barbarian child she had been. And he certainly could not blame her for rejecting her parents as completely as they had abandoned her. He wondered if she understood why she drove herself so hard, for she was trying to prove herself to people who would never know her accomplishments, and never care. Perhaps some day she would prove herself to herself and be free of the last shackles binding her to her past.

"Hmm, yes," Kirk said, pulling Spock back from his reflections. "I do recall that Vulcans are renowned for their ability to be idle."

Spock decided to change the subject himself. He picked up the package he had retrieved before coming into the debriefing room. Feeling somewhat awkward, he offered it to Kirk.

"What's this?" Jim asked.

"It is," Spock said, "a birthday present."

Jim took the gift and turned it over in his hands. "How in the world did you know it was my birthday?"

"The date is not difficult to ascertain."

"I mean, why—? No, never mind, another silly question. Thank you, Spock."

"Perhaps you should open it before you thank me; it may not strike your fancy."

"I'm sure it will—but you know what they say: It's the thought that counts." He slid his fingers beneath the outside edge of the elegantly folded paper.

"I have indeed heard the saying, and I have always wanted to ask," Spock said, with honest curiosity, "if it is the thought that counts, why do humans bother with the gift?"

Jim laughed. "There's no good answer to that. I guess it's just an example of the distance between our ideals and reality."

The parcel was wrapped in paper only, with no adhesive or ties. After purchasing the gift, Spock had passed a small booth at which an elderly woman created simple, striking packages with nothing but folded paper. Fascinated by the geometry and topology of what she was doing, Spock watched for some time, and then had her wrap Jim's birthday present.

At a touch, the wrapping fanned away untorn.

Jim saw what was inside and sat down heavily.

"Perhaps . . . it *is* the thought that counts," Spock said.

"No, Spock, good Lord, it's beautiful." He touched the leather binding with one finger; he picked the book up in both hands and opened it gently, slowly, being careful of its spine.

"I only recently became aware of your fondness for antiques," Spock said. It was a liking he had begun to believe he understood, in an odd way, once he paid attention to it. The book, for example, combined the flaws and perfections of something handmade; it was curiously satisfying.

"Thank you, Spock. I like it very much." He let a few pages flip past and read the novel's first line. " 'It was the best of times, it was the worst of times . . .' Hmm, are you trying to tell me something?"

"Not from the text," Spock said, "and with the book itself, only happy birthday. Does that not qualify as 'the best of times'?"

Jim looked uncomfortable, and he avoided Spock's gaze. Spock wondered how a gift that had at first brought pleasure could so quickly turn into a matter of awkwardness. Once again he had the feeling that Jim Kirk was deeply unhappy about something.

"Jim—?"

"Thank you, Spock, very much," Kirk said, cutting Spock off and ignoring the question in his voice. "I mean it. Look, I know you have to get back to the *Enterprise*. I'll see you tomorrow."

And with that, he was gone.

Spock picked up the bit of textured wrapping paper and refolded it into its original shape, around empty air.

He wondered if he would ever begin to understand human beings.

Chapter 2

Log Entry by Commander Pavel Chekov, Duty Officer. U.S.S. *Reliant* on orbital approach to Alpha Ceti VI, continuing our search for a planet to serve as a test site for the Genesis experiment. This will be the sixteenth world we have visited; so far, our attempts to fulfill all the requirements for the test site have met with failure.

Reliant—better known to its crew, not necessarily fondly, as "this old bucket"—plowed through space toward Alpha Ceti and its twenty small, uninhabited, undistinguished, unexplored planets. Pavel Chekov, on duty on the elderly ship's bridge, finished his log report and ordered the computer to seal it.

"Log complete, Captain," he said.

"Thank you, Mr. Chekov." Clark Terrell leaned back in the captain's seat. "Is the probe data for Alpha Ceti on-line?"

"Aye, sir." Chekov keyed the data to the viewscreen so that Captain Terrell could display it if he chose. For now, the screen showed Alpha Ceti VI. The planet spun slowly before them, its surface smudged blurrily in shades of sickly yellow. Nitrogen and sulfur oxides dominated its atmosphere, and the sand that covered it had been ground and blasted from its crust by eons of corrosive, high-velocity winds.

Alpha Ceti VI was a place where one would not

expect to find life. If the crew of *Reliant* were lucky, this time their expectations would be met.

And about time, too, Chekov thought. We need a little luck.

At the beginning of this voyage, Chekov had expected it to be boring, but short and easy. How difficult could it be to find a planet with no life? Now, several months later, he felt as if he were trapped in a journey that was boring, unending, and impossible. Lifeless planets abounded, but lifeless worlds of the right size, orbiting the proper sort of star, within the star's biosphere, in a star system otherwise uninhabited: such planets were not so easy to discover. They had inspected fifteen promisingly barren worlds, but each in its turn had somehow violated the strict parameters of the experimental conditions.

Chekov was bored. The whole crew was bored.

At first, the ship had traveled to worlds at least superficially documented by previous research teams, but *Reliant* now had begun to go farther afield, to places seldom if ever visited by crewed Federation craft. The computer search Chekov had done on the Alpha Ceti system turned up no official records except the ancient survey of an automated probe. He had been mildly surprised to find so little data, then mildly surprised again to have thought he had ever heard of the system. Alpha Ceti VI had come up on the list of Genesis candidates for exactly the same reason no one had bothered to visit it after the probe report of sixty years before: it was monumentally uninteresting.

Terrell displayed the probe data as a corner overlay on the viewscreen and added a companion block of the information they had collected on the way in.

"I see what you mean about the discrepancies, Pavel," he said. He considered the screen and stroked the short black hair of his curly beard.

The probe data showed twenty planets: fourteen small, rocky inner ones; three gas giants; three outer eccentrics. But what *Reliant* saw on approach was nineteen planets, only thirteen of them inner ones.

"I've been working on that, Captain," Chekov said, "and there are two possibilities. Alpha Ceti was surveyed by one of the earliest probes: their data wasn't always completely reliable, and some of the archival preservation has been pretty sloppy. It's also possible that the system's gone through some alteration since the probe's visit."

"Doesn't sound too likely."

"Well, no, sir." Sixty years was an infinitesimal distance in the past, astronomically speaking; the chances of any noticeable change occurring since then were very small. "Probe error is a fairly common occurrence, Captain."

Terrell glanced back and grinned. "You mean maybe we think we're headed for a ball of rock, and we'll find a garden spot instead?"

"*Bozhe moi!*" Chekov said. "My God, I hope not. No, sir, our new scans confirm the originals on the planet itself. Rock, sand, corrosive atmosphere."

"Three cheers for the corrosive atmosphere," Mr. Beach said, and everybody on the bridge laughed.

"I agree one hundred percent, Mr. Beach," Terrell said. "Take us in."

Several hours later, on orbital approach, Chekov watched the viewscreen intently, willing the ugly little planet to be the one they were looking for. He had had enough of this trip. There was too little work and too much time with nothing to do. It encouraged paranoia and depression, which he had been feeling with distressing intensity on this leg of their voyage. On occasion, he even wondered if his being assigned here were due to something worse than bad luck. Could it be punishment for some inadvertent mistake, or the unspoken dislike of some superior officer—?

He kept telling himself the idea was foolish and,

worse, one that could become self-fulfilling if he let it take him over and sour him.

Besides, if he were being punished it only made sense to assume others in the crew were, too. Yet a crew of troublemakers produced disaffection and disillusion: the ship was free of such problems. Or anyway it had been until they pulled this intolerable assignment.

Besides, Captain Terrell had an excellent reputation: he was not the sort of officer generally condemned to command a bunch of dead-enders. He was soft-spoken and easygoing; if the days stretching into weeks stretching into months of fruitless search troubled him, he did not show the stress. He was no James Kirk, but . . .

Maybe that's what's wrong, Chekov thought. I've been thinking about the old days on the *Enterprise* too much lately and comparing them to what I'm doing now. And what I'm doing now simply does not compare.

But, then—what would?

"Standard orbit, Mr. Beach," Captain Terrell said.

"Standard orbit, sir," the helm officer replied.

"What do we have on the surface scan?"

"No change, Captain."

Chekov got a signal on his screen that he wished he could pretend he had not noticed.

"Except . . ."

"Oh, no," somebody groaned.

Every crew member on the bridge turned to stare at Chekov with one degree or another of disbelief, irritation, or animosity. On the other side of the upper bridge, the communications officer muttered a horrible curse.

Chekov glanced down at Terrell. The captain hunched his shoulders, then forced himself to relax. "Don't tell me you've got something," he said. He rose and came up the stairs to look at Chekov's data.

It *is* getting to him, Chekov thought. Even him.

"It's only a minor energy flux," Chekov said, trying

to blunt the impact of his finding. "It doesn't necessarily mean there's biological activity down there."

"I've heard that line before," Terrell said. "What are the chances that the scanner's out of adjustment?"

"I just checked it out, sir," Chekov said. "Twice." He immediately wished he had not added that last remark.

"Maybe it's pre-biotic," Beach said.

Terrell chuckled. "Come on, Stoney. That's something we've been through before, too. Of all the things Marcus won't go for, tampering with pre-biotics is probably top of the list."

"Maybe it's *pre*-pre-biotic," Beach said wryly.

This time nobody laughed.

"All right, get Dr. Marcus on the horn. At least we can suggest transplantation. Again."

Chekov shook his head. "You know what she'll say."

On the Regulus I Laboratory Space Station, Dr. Carol Marcus listened, frowning, as Captain Terrell relayed the information *Reliant* had collected so far.

"You know my feelings about disturbing a pre-biotic system," she said. "I won't be a party to it. The long-range—"

"Dr. Marcus, the long range you're talking about is millions of years!"

"Captain, *we* were pre-biotic millions of years ago. Where would we be if somebody had come along when Earth was a volcanic hell-pit, and said, 'Well, *this* will never amount to anything, let's mess around with it'?"

"Probably we wouldn't care," Terrell said.

Carol Marcus grinned. "You have it exactly. Please don't waste your time trying to change my mind about this; it simply isn't a matter for debate."

She watched his reaction: he was less than happy with her answer.

"Captain, the project won't be ready for the next stage of the test for at least three months. There's no pressure on you to find a place for it instantaneously—" She stopped; the unflappable Clark Terrell looked like he was about to start tearing out his very curly, handsomely graying black hair. "Wrong thing to say, huh?"

"Doctor, we've spent a long time looking for a place that would fit your requirements. I'd match my crew against any in Starfleet. They're good people. But if I put them through three more months of this, I'll have a mutiny on my hands. They can take boredom—but what they've got is paralysis!"

"I see," Marcus said.

"Look, suppose what our readings indicate is the end of an evolutionary line rather than the beginning? What if some microbes here are about to go extinct? Just barely hanging on. Would you approve transplantation then?"

"I can't do that," she said. She chewed absently on her thumbnail but stopped abruptly. You're a little old to still be chewing your nails, Carol, she thought. You ought at least to have cut it out when you turned forty.

Maybe when I hit fifty, she replied to herself.

"Don't you leave *any* room for compromise?" Terrell asked angrily.

"Wait, Captain," she said. "I'm sorry, I didn't mean that the way it sounded. It isn't that I wouldn't give you a go-ahead. It's that finding a species endangered by its own environment is a fairly common occurrence. There are established channels for deciding whether to transplant, and established places to take the species to."

"A microbial zoo, eh?"

"Not just microbes, but that's the idea."

"What kind of time-frame are we talking about?" Terrell asked cautiously.

"Do you mean how long will you have to wait before the endangered species subcommittee gives an approval?"

"What's what I *asked*."

"They're used to acting quickly—if they don't it's

34

often too late. They need documentation, though. Why don't you go down and have a look?"

"We're on our way!"

"I don't want to give you false hopes," Marcus said quickly. "If you find so much as a pre-biotic spherule, a pseudo-membranous configuration, even a viroid aggregate, the show's off. On the other hand, if you have discovered an evolutionary line in need of preservation, not only will you have found a Genesis site, you'll probably get a commendation."

"I'll settle for the Genesis site," Terrell said.

His image faded.

Carol Marcus sighed. She wished she were on board *Reliant* to keep an eye on what they were doing. But her work on Genesis was at too delicate a point; she had to stay with it. Clark Terrell had given her no reason to distrust him. But he was obviously less than thrilled about having been assigned to do fetch-and-carry work for her laboratory. He was philosophically indifferent to her requirements for the Genesis site, while she was ethically committed to them. She could imagine how *Reliant*'s crew referred to her and the other scientists in the lab: a bunch of ivory-tower eggheads, test-tube jugglers, fantasy-world dreamers.

She sighed again.

"Mother, why do you let them pull that stuff on you?"

"Hello, David," she said. "I didn't hear you come in."

Her son joined her by the communications console.

"They're lazy," he said.

"They're bored. And if they've found something that really does need to be transplanted . . ."

"Come on, mother, it's the military mentality. 'Never put off tomorrow what you can put off today.' If life is beginning to evolve there—"

"I know, I know," Carol said. "I'm the one who wrote the specs—remember?"

"Hey, mother, take it easy. It's going to work."

"That's the trouble, I think. It *is* going to work, and I'm a little frightened of what will happen when it does."

"What will happen is that you'll be remembered along with Newton, Einstein, Surak—"

"More likely Darwin, and I'll probably get as much posthumous flak, too."

"Listen, they might not even wait till you're dead to start with the flak."

"Thanks a lot!" Carol said with mock outrage. "I don't know what I can hope for from other people; I can't even get any respect from my own offspring."

"That's me, an ingrate all the way." He gave her a quick hug. "Want to team up for bridge after dinner?"

"Maybe. . . ." She was still preoccupied by her conversation with Terrell.

"Yeah," David said. "Every time we have to deal with Starfleet, I get nervous, too."

"There's so much risk. . . ." Carol said softly.

"Every discovery worth making has had the potential to be perverted into a dreadful weapon."

"My goodness, that sounds familiar," Carol said.

David grinned. "It ought to, it's what you've been telling me for twenty years." Serious again, he said, "We just have to make damned certain that the military doesn't take Genesis away from you. There're some who'll try, that's for sure. That overgrown boy scout you used to hang out with—"

"Listen, kiddo," Carol said, "Jim Kirk was a lot of things . . . but he was *never* a boy scout." Her son was the last person she wanted to talk about Jim Kirk with. She gestured toward the file David was carrying. "Last night's batch?"

"Yeah, fresh out of the machine." He opened the file of X-ray micrographs, and they set to work.

Jim Kirk pulled the reading light closer, shifted uncomfortably on his living room couch, held the book

Spock had given him closer to his eyes, then held it at arm's length. No matter what he did, his eyes refused to focus on the small print.

I'm just tired, he thought.

It was true: he was tired. But that was not the reason he could not read his book.

He closed it carefully, set it on the table beside him, and lay back on the couch. He could see the pictures on the far wall of the room quite clearly, even down to the finest lines on the erotic Kvern black-and-white that was one of his proudest possessions. He had owned the small drawing for a long time; it used to hang in his cabin back on the *Enterprise*.

A few of his antiques were alien artifacts, collected offworld, but in truth he preferred work from his own culture, particularly England's Victorian era. He wondered if Spock knew that, or if the Dickens first edition were a lucky guess.

Spock, making a lucky guess? He would be horrified. Jim grinned.

Only in the last ten years or so had the beauty of antiques overcome his reluctance to gather too many possessions, to be weighed down by *things*. It was a long time since he had been able to pick up and leave with one small suitcase and no glance back. Sometimes he wished he could return to those days, but it was impossible. He was an admiral. He had too many other responsibilities.

The doorbell chimed.

Jim started and sat up. It was rather late for visitors.

"Come," he said. The apartment's sensors responded to his voice. Leonard McCoy came in, with a smile and an armful of packages.

"Why, Doctor," Jim said, surprised. "What errant transporter beamed you to my doorstep?"

McCoy struck a pose. "'*Quidquid id est, timeo Danaos et dona ferentes,*'" he said.

"How's that again?"

37

"Well, that's the original. What people usually say these days is 'Beware Romulans bearing gifts.' Not quite the same, but it seemed appropriate, considering—" he rummaged around in one of the packages and drew out a bottle full of electric-blue liquid, "—this. Happy birthday." He handed Jim the chunky, asymmetric bottle.

"Romulan ale—? Bones, this stuff is so illegal—"

"I only use it for medicinal purposes. Don't be a prig."

Jim squinted at the label. "Twenty-two . . . eighty-three?"

"It takes the stuff a while to ferment. Give it here."

Jim handed it back, opened the glass-paneled doors of the cherry-wood Victorian secretary where he kept his dishes, and took out a couple of beer mugs. McCoy poured them both full.

"Is it my imagination, or is it smoking?"

McCoy laughed. "Considering the brew, quite possibly both." He clinked his glass against Jim's. "Cheers." He took a deep swallow.

Jim sipped cautiously. It was a long time since he had drunk Romulan ale, but not so long that he had forgotten what a kick it packed.

Its electric hue was appropriate; he felt the jolt of the first taste, as if the active ingredient skipped the digestive system completely and headed straight for the brain.

"Wow," he said. He drank again, more deeply, savoring both the taste and the effect.

"Now open this one." McCoy handed him a package which, rather than being stuffed into a brown paper bag, was gilt-wrapped.

Jim took the package, turned it over in his hand, and shook it.

"I'm almost afraid to. What is it?" He took another swallow of the ale, a real swallow this time, and fumbled at the shiny silver tissue. Strange: he had not had any trouble opening Spock's present this afternoon. A tremendously funny idea struck him. "Is it a tribble?" He started to laugh. "Or maybe some contraband Klingon—"

"It's another antique for your collection," McCoy said. "Your health!" He lifted his glass and drank again.

"Come on, Bones, what is it?" He got one end of the package free.

"Nope, you gotta open it."

Though his hands were beginning to feel as if he were wearing gloves, Jim could feel a hard, spidery shape. He gave up trying to get the wrapping off in one piece and tore it away. "I know what it is, it's—" He squinted at the gold and glass construction, glanced at McCoy, and looked down at his present again. "Well, it's . . . charming."

"They're four hundred years old. You don't find many with the lenses still intact."

"Uh, Bones . . . what are they?"

"Spectacles."

Jim drank more ale. Maybe if he caught up with McCoy he would be able to figure out what he was talking about.

"For your eyes," McCoy said. "They're almost as good as Retinax Five—"

"But I'm *allergic* to Retinax," Jim said petulantly. After the buildup the doctor gave about restoring the flexibility of his eyes with the drug, Jim had been rather put out when he turned out to be unable to tolerate it.

"Exactly!" McCoy refilled both their glasses. "*Happy birth*day!"

Jim discovered that the spectacles unfolded. A curve of gold wire connected two little half-rounds of glass; hinged hooks attached to each side.

"No, look, here, like this." McCoy slid one hook behind each of Jim's ears. The wire curve rested on his nose, holding the bits of glass beneath his eyes.

"They're spectacles. Oh, and I was only kidding about the lenses being antique. They're designed for your eyes."

Jim remembered a picture in an old book he had. He lowered the spectacles on the bridge of his nose.

"That's it," McCoy said. "Look at me, over the top. Now look down, through the lenses. You ought to be able to read comfortably with those."

Jim got them in the right position, did as McCoy said, and blinked with surprise. He picked up Spock's book, opened it, and found the tiny print in perfect focus.

"That's amazing! Bones, I don't know what to say. . . ."

"Say thank you."

"Thank you," Jim said obediently.

"Now have another drink." McCoy drained the bottle into their mugs.

They sat and drank. The Romulan ale continued to perform up to its usual standard. Jim felt a bit as he had the first time he ever experienced zero gee—queasy and confused. He could not think of anything to say, though the silence felt heavy and awkward. Several times McCoy seemed on the verge of speaking, and several times he stopped. Jim had the feeling that whatever the doctor was working up to, he would prefer not to hear. He scowled into his glass. Now he was getting paranoid. Knowing it was the result of the drink did nothing to relieve his distress.

"Damn it, Jim," McCoy said suddenly. "What the hell's the matter? Everybody has birthdays. Why are we treating yours like a funeral?"

"Is *that* why you came over here?" Jim snapped. "I really don't want a lecture."

"Then what *do* you want? What are you doing, sitting here all alone on your birthday? And don't give me that crap about 'games for the young' again, either! That's a crock, and you know it. This has nothing to do with age. It has to do with you jockeying a computer console instead of flying your ship through the galaxy!"

"Spare me your notions of poetry, please. I've got a job to do—"

"Bull. You never should have given up the *Enterprise* after Voyager."

Jim took another drink of Romulan ale, wishing the first fine glow had lasted longer. Now he remembered why he had never developed a taste for this stuff. The high at the beginning was almost good enough to compensate for the depression at the end. Almost, but not quite.

He chuckled sadly. "Yeah, I'd've made a great pirate, Bones."

"That's bull, too. If you'd made a few waves, they wouldn't have had any choice but to reassign you."

"There's hardly a flag officer in Starfleet who wouldn't rather be flying than pushing bytes from one data bank to another."

"We're not talking about every flag officer in Starfleet. We're talking about James T. Kirk—"

"—who has a certain amount of notoriety. It wouldn't be fair to trade on that—"

"Jim, ethics are one thing, but you're crucifying yourself on yours!"

"There are rules, and regulations—"

"Which you are hiding behind."

"Oh yeah? And what am I hiding from?"

"From yourself—Admiral."

Jim held back an angry reply. After a long pause he said, "I have a feeling you're going to give me more advice, whether I want it or not."

"Jim, I don't know if I think this is more important because I'm your doctor, or because I'm your friend. Get your ship back. Get it back before you really do get old. Before you turn into part of your own collection."

Jim swirled the dregs of his drink around in his glass, then looked up and met McCoy's gaze.

The wind nearly knocked Chekov over as soon as he lost the protection of the transporter beam. Alpha Ceti

VI was one of the nastiest, most inhospitable places he had ever been. Alpha Ceti VI was worse even than Siberia in the winter.

Driven by the storm, the sand screamed against his pressure suit. Captain Terrell materialized beside him, looked around, and opened a channel to *Reliant*.

"Terrell to *Reliant*."

"*Reliant*. Beach here, Captain." The transmission wavered. "Pretty poor reception, sir."

"It will do, Stoney. We're down. No evidence of life—or anything else."

"I copy, sir."

"Look, I don't want to listen to this static all afternoon. I'll call you, say, every half hour."

". . . Aye, sir."

Kyle broke in. "Remember about staying in the open, Captain."

"Don't fuss, Mr. Kyle. Terrell out." He shut down the transmission and turned on his tricorder.

Chekov stretched out his arm; his hand almost disappeared in the heavy blowing sand. Even if whatever they were seeking were macroscopic, rather than microbial, they would never find it visually. He, too, began scanning for the signal that had brought them to the surface of this wretched world.

"You getting anything, Pavel?"

Chekov could barely make out the captain's words, not because the transmission was faulty but because the wind and the sand were so loud they drowned out his voice.

"No, sir, nothing yet."

"You're sure these are the right coordinates?"

"Remember that garden spot you mentioned, Captain? Well, this is it." Chekov took a few steps forward. Sand ground and squealed in the joints of his suit. They could not afford to stay on the surface very long, for these conditions would degrade even an almost indestructible material. Chekov knew what would happen if his suit were torn or punctured. The oxides of sulfur that formed so much of the atmosphere would contaminate his air and dissolve in the moisture in his lungs. Chekov intended to die in some far more pleasant way than by breathing sulfuric and sulfurous acids: some far more pleasant way, and some far more distant time in the future.

"I can't see a damned thing," Terrell said. He started off toward the slight rise the tricorder indicated. Chekov trudged after him. The wind tried to push him faster than he could comfortably walk in the treacherous sand.

Sweat ran down the sides of his face; his nose itched. No one yet had invented a pressure suit in which one could both use one's hands and scratch one's nose.

"I'm getting nothing, Captain," Chekov said. Nothing but one case of creeps. "Let's go."

He got no reply. He looked up. At the top of the hillock, Captain Terrell stood staring before him, his form vague and blurry in the sand. He gestured quickly. Chekov struggled up the sand dune, trying to run, sliding on the slick, sharp grains. He reached Terrell's side and stopped, astonished.

The sand dune formed a windbreak for the small hollow before them, a sort of storm's eye of clearer air. Chekov could see perhaps a hundred meters.

In that hundred meters lay a half-buried group of ruined buildings.

Suddenly he shivered.

"Whatever it is," Clark Terrell said, "it isn't pre-biotic." He stepped over the knife-sharp crest of the dune and slid down its concave leeward side.

After a moment, reluctantly, Chekov followed. The unpleasant feeling of apprehension that had teased and disturbed him ever since they started for Alpha Ceti gripped him tighter, growing toward dread.

Terrell passed the first structure. Chekov discarded any hope that they might have come upon some weird formation of violent wind and alien geology. What they had found was the wreckage of a spaceship.

Chekov would have been willing to bet that it was a human-made spaceship, too. Its lines were familiar. Alien craft always appeared . . . alien.

"These look like cargo carriers," Terrell said.

Chekov leaned over to put his faceplate against a porthole, trying to see inside the ruined ship.

A child popped up, laughed silently, and disappeared.

"Bozhe moi!" Chekov cried, starting violently. He fell backward into the sand.

"Chekov! What the hell—?" Terrell stumbled toward him.

"Face! I saw—face of child!"

He pointed, but the porthole was empty.

Terrell helped him to his feet. "Come on. This place is getting to you."

"But I *saw* it," Chekov said.

"Look, there's the airlock. Let's check it out."

"Captain, I have bad feeling—I think we should go back to *Reliant* and look for different test site and pretend we never came here. Lenin himself said 'better part of valor is discretion.' "

"Come along," Terrell said. His tone forbade argument. "And anyway, it was Shakespeare."

"No, Captain, Lenin. Perhaps other fellow—" Chekov stopped and reminded himself of the way Standard was constructed. "Perhaps the other fellow stole it."

Terrell laughed, but even that did not make Chekov feel any easier.

Though sand half covered most of the cargo modules, testifying to some considerable time since the crash, the airlock operated smoothly. In this environment, that was possible only if the mechanism had been maintained.

Chekov hung back. "Captain, I don't think we should go in there. Mr. Kyle's warning—" The electrical disturbances in the atmosphere that had disrupted communications and made scanning so difficult gave problems to the transporter as well; Kyle had said that even a covering of tree branches, or a roof (knowing what they expected to find, Chekov and Terrell had both laughed at that caution), could change beaming up from "just barely possible" to "out of the question."

"Mr. Kyle has one flaw," Terrell said, "and that is that he invariably errs far on the side of caution. Are you coming?"

"I'll go in, Captain," Chekov said reluctantly. "But you stay outside, *pozhalusta,* and keep in contact with ship."

"Pavel, this is ridiculous. Calm down. I can tell you're upset—"

On *Reliant,* Chekov occasionally got teased for losing his Standard, in which he was ordinarily fluent, when he was angry or very tired.

Or—though his shipmates had no way of knowing this—when he was terrified.

"Look," Terrell said. "I'll go in. If you want to, you can stay out here on guard."

Chekov knew that he could not let Terrell enter the cargo ship alone. Unwillingly he followed the captain into the airlock.

The inner doors slid open. Chekov had to wait a moment, but after his eyes adjusted to the dimness he saw beds and tables, a book, an empty coffee cup: people lived here. They must have survived the crash of the cargo ship. But where were they?

"We've got a breathable atmosphere," Terrell said. He unfastened his helmet. Chekov glanced at his tricorder. Terrell was right: the proportions of oxygen, nitrogen, and carbon dioxide were all normal, and there was barely a trace of the noxious chemicals that made up the outside air. Even so, Chekov opened his helmet seal half expecting the burning pungency of acid vapors.

But the place smelled like every dormitory Chekov had ever been in: of sweat and dirty socks.

Outside, the wind scattered sand against the walls. Terrell went farther into the reconverted cargo hold.

His footsteps echoed. There were no sounds of habitation; yet the place did not *feel* deserted.

It felt evil.

"What the hell is all this? Did they crash? And where are they?"

Terrell stopped in the entrance to the next chamber, a kitchen.

On the stove, a faint cloud of steam rose from a pot of stew.

Chekov stared at it.

"Captain . . ."

Terrell was gone. Chekov hurried after him, entering a laboratory, where Terrell poked around among the equipment. He stopped near a large glass tank full of sand. Chekov went toward him, hoping to persuade him to return to the ship, or at least call in a well-armed security team.

"Christ!"

Terrell leaped away from the tank.

Chekov ripped his phaser from the suit's outer clip and crouched, waiting, ready, but there was nothing to fire at.

"Captain—what—?"

"There's something in that damned tank!" He approached it cautiously, his hand on his own phaser.

The sand roiled like water. A long shape cut a stroke across the surface, and Chekov flinched back.

"It's all right," Terrell said. "It's just some kind of animal or—"

The quiet gurgle of a child, talking to itself, playing with sounds, cut him off as effectively as a shout or a scream.

"I told you!" Chekov cried. "I told you I saw—"

"Shh." Terrell started toward the sound, motioning Chekov to follow.

Chekov obeyed, trying to calm himself. So what if there were a child? This was not a world where Chekov would wish to father and try to raise a baby, but obviously at least one couple among the survivors of the cargo ship crash had felt differently. Chekov's fear was reasonless, close to cowardice—

He stepped through a crumpled and deformed passageway and peered into the next chamber.

The crash had twisted the room around, leaving it tumbled on its side, one wall now the floor, the floor and ceiling now walls. The change made the proportions odd and disconcerting; worse, the floor was not quite flat, the walls not quite straight.

All alone, in the middle of the room, sitting on the floor—the wall—the baby reached out to them and gurgled and giggled with joy. Terrell climbed down from the sideways entrance and approached the child tentatively.

"Well, kid, hi, didn't your folks even leave a baby-sitter?"

Chekov looked around the room. The wall that had become the ceiling displayed a collection of sharp, shining swords; Chekov recognized only the wavy-bladed kris. He recognized few of the titles of the books on a shelf nearby: *King Lear?* That sounded like imperialist propaganda to him. *Bible?* Twentieth-century mythology, if he recalled correctly.

And then he saw, hanging from the floor-wall, the ship's insignia, and the reason for his terror came at him in a crushing blow.

Botany Bay.

"*Bozhe moi!*" Chekov whispered. "*Botany Bay*, no, it can't be. . . ."

Terrell chucked the baby gently under the chin with his forefinger. "What'd you say, Pavel?"

Chekov lunged forward, grabbed Terrell by the shoulder, and dragged him toward the passageway.

"Wait a minute! What's the matter with you?"

"We've got to get out of here! Now! Captain, please trust me, hurry!"

He forcibly pushed the bigger man up and through the hatch and climbed after him. Angry now, Terrell tried to turn back.

"But the child—"

"I can't explain now!" Chekov cried. "No time! Hurry!" He pushed the captain down the battered companionway, which was too narrow to allow Terrell to put up much struggle. Chekov fumbled with his helmet, got it fastened, and turned on the suit's communicator.

"Chekov to *Reliant,* come in *Reliant.* Mayday, mayday—"

Static answered his pleas.

By the time they reached the laboratory, Terrell had caught his urgency or decided to humor him now and bust him back to ensign later—Chekov did not care which. Terrell put on his helmet and fastened it as they reached the kitchen and ran into the connecting hall. The dormitory was still deserted. Chekov began to hope they might get outside and contact the ship in time. They plunged into the airlock. Chekov continued to call *Reliant,* hoping to get through, determined to reach it the instant he and Terrell left the building.

The door opened. Chekov bolted forward.

He stopped.

They were surrounded by suited figures, each one armed, and every weapon pointed straight at them.

"Beam us up!" Chekov cried into his transmitter.

As he grabbed at his phaser, one of the suited figures lunged forward, disarmed him, and knocked him back into the airlock.

High above, in *Reliant,* Mr. Kyle tried again to raise Terrell and Chekov. They had only been out of touch for a little while, true, but the conditions were so terrible on the surface of Alpha Ceti VI that he would have preferred continuous contact.

"Try again," Beach said unnecessarily.

"*Reliant* to Captain Terrell, Kyle here. Do you copy, Captain Terrell? Come in, Captain, please respond. . . ."

He got no reply.

Beach let out his breath in an irritated snort.

"Let's give them a little more time."

Kyle knew as well as Beach did how much Clark Terrell hated to be second-guessed; nevertheless, he was about to protest when a sudden squawk came through his headphone and echoed on the speakers. He flinched.

"What was that?" Beach said. "Did you hear it?"

"I heard it." He channeled the transmission through the computer, enhancing and filtering it. "Stoney, I want to put more power to the sensors."

"You already overrode the alarm—much more and you'll blow out the circuits completely."

"I think they're in trouble."

The transmission returned from enhancement.

"Eeeeebeeeesssss . . ." squealed out of the speaker. Kyle slapped his console and forced the signal through the program again.

"Beeeeeeussss . . ."

And again.

Though flattened and distorted, it was Chekov's voice.

"Beam us . . ."

Kyle looked up at Beach.

"Beam us . . ."

"Okay—more power," Beach said. "Get a lock on them!"

"Beam us . . ."

"Beam us . . ."

"Beam us . . ."

Chapter 3

When Captain Terrell tried to explain that he and Chekov had been looking for survivors, that they were, in effect, a rescue party, one of the survivors expressed gratitude by backhanding him with the full weight of body and arm and massive suit glove. Terrell sagged.

Chekov did not try to protest their capture. He knew the attempt would be futile.

He and Terrell still wore their suits, though their helmets and phasers had been taken. Escape seemed impossible. Besides the four people holding them, twelve or fifteen others stood in silence around them.

As if they were waiting.

Chekov felt more frightened of what—whom—they were waiting for than of all of them together. Without actually looking at his phaser, Chekov set himself to get to it. He forced himself to relax; he pretended to give up. When in response one of his captors just slightly relaxed the hold, Chekov lunged forward.

He was not fast enough. His hands were jammed up under his shoulder blades, twisting his arms painfully. He cried out. Terrell's captors jerked him upright, too, though he was still half-stunned.

Chekov had no other chance to resist. The pressure on his arms did not ease: it intensified. Through a haze of pain, he sought desperately through old memories to recall everything he could about *Botany Bay*. So much had happened in so short a time that while he remembered the incident itself with terrible clarity, some of the details had blurred. It was a long time ago, too, fifteen years . . .

The airlock hummed into a cycle. The guards forced Chekov to attention, pulled Terrell upright, and turned them both to face the doorway. The bruise on Terrell's face was deep red against his black skin. Sweat ran down Chekov's sides.

A tall figure, silhouetted by the light, paused, stepped out of the chamber, and slowly, deliberately, removed its helmet.

Chekov's breath sighed out in a soft, desperate moan.

"Khan. . . ."

The man had changed: he appeared far more than fifteen years older. His long hair was now white, streaked with iron gray. But the aura of power and self-assurance was undiminished; the changes meant nothing. Chekov recognized him instantly.

Khan Singh glanced toward him; only then did Chekov realize he had spoken the name aloud. Khan's dark, direct gaze made the blood drain from Chekov's face.

Khan approached and looked them over. The unrelenting inspection shocked Terrell fully back to consciousness, but Khan dismissed him with a shrug.

"I don't know you," he said. He turned toward Chekov, who shrank away.

"But *you*," he said softly, gently, "I remember you, Mr. Chekov. I never hoped to see *you* again."

Chekov closed his eyes to shut out the sight of Khan's terrifying expression, which was very near a smile.

"Chekov, who is this man?" Terrell tried vainly to reassert some authority.

"He was . . . experiment, Captain. And criminal." Though he feared angering Khan, he could think of no other way, and no satisfactory way at all, to describe him. "He's from . . . twentieth century." He was an experiment, a noble dream gone wrong. Genetic engineering had enhanced his vast intelligence; nature had conveyed upon him great presence and charisma. What had caused his overwhelming need for power, Pavel Chekov did not know.

Khan Singh's only reaction to Chekov's statement was a slow smile.

"What's the meaning of this treatment?" Terrell said angrily. "I demand—"

"You, sir, are in a position to demand nothing." Khan's voice was very mild. He could be charming—Chekov recalled that all too well. "I, on the other hand, am in a position to grant nothing." He gestured to the people, to the surroundings. "You see here all that remains of the crew of my ship, *Botany Bay,* indeed all that remains of the ship itself, marooned here fifteen years ago by Captain James T. Kirk."

The words were simply explanatory, but the tone was chilling.

"I can grant nothing, for we have nothing," Khan said.

Terrell appealed to Khan's ragtag group of men and women.

"Listen to me, you people—"

"Save your strength, Captain," Khan said. "They have been sworn to me, and I to them, since two hundred years before you were born. We owe each other our lives." He glanced kindly at Chekov. "My dear Mr. Chekov, do you mean you never told him the tale?" He returned his attention to Terrell. "Do you mean James Kirk never amused you by telling the story of how he 'rescued' my ship and its company from the cryogenic prison of deep space? He never made sport of us in public? Captain, I'm touched."

His words were filled with quiet, deadly venom.

"I don't even know Admiral Kirk!"

"*Admiral* Kirk? Ah, so he gained a reward for his brave deeds and his acts of chivalry—for exiling seventy people to a barren heap of sand!"

"You lie!" Chekov shouted. "I saw the world we left

you on! It was beautiful; it was like a garden—flowers, fruit trees, streams . . . and its moon!" Chekov remembered the moon most clearly, an enormous silver globe hanging over the land, ten times the size of the moon on Earth, for Captain Kirk had left Khan and his followers on one of a pair of worlds, a twin system in which planet and satellite were of a size. But one was living, the other lifeless.

"Yes," Khan said, in a rough whisper. "Alpha Ceti V was that, for a while."

Chekov gasped. *"Alpha Ceti V!"* The name came back, and all the pieces fell into place: no official records, for fear Khan Singh would free himself again; the discrepancies between the probe records and the data *Reliant* collected. Now, too late, Chekov understood why he had lived the last few days under an increasing pall of dread.

"My child," Khan said, his tone hurt, "did you forget? Did you forget where you left me? You did, I see . . . ah, you ordinaries with your pitiful memories."

If the twin worlds had still existed, Chekov would have seen them on approach and remembered, and warned Terrell away.

"Why did you leave Alpha Ceti V for its twin?" Chekov asked. "What happened to it?"

"This is Alpha Ceti V!" Khan cried.

Chekov stared at him, confused.

Khan lowered his voice again, but his deep black eyes retained their dangerous glitter.

"Alpha Ceti VI, our beautiful moon—you did not survey that, did you, Mr. Chekov? You never bothered to note its tectonic instability. It exploded, Mr. Chekov. It exploded! It laid waste to our planet. *I* enabled us to survive, I, with nothing to work with but the trivial contents of these cargo holds."

"Captain Kirk was your host—" Chekov said.

"And he never appreciated the honor fate offered him. I was a prince on Earth; I stood before millions and led them. He could not bear the thought that I might return to power. He could only conquer me by playing at being a god. His Zeus to my Prometheus: he put me here, in adamantine chains, to guard a barren rock!"

"You tried to steal his ship—"

Ignoring his words, Khan bent down and looked straight into Pavel Chekov's eyes. "Are you his eagle, Mr. Chekov? Did you come to tear out my entrails?"

"—and you tried to murder him!"

Khan turned away, and gazed at Clark Terrell. "What of you, Captain? Perhaps you are my Chiron. Did you come to take my place in purgatory?"

"I . . . I don't know what you mean," Terrell said.

"No, you do not! You know nothing of sacrifice. Not you, not James T. Kirk—" he snarled the name, "—no one but the courageous Lieutenant McGiver, who defied your precious admiral, who gave up everything to join me in exile."

Khan's voice broke, and he fell silent. He turned away.

"A plague upon you all."

He swung around on them again. His eyes were bright with tears, but his self-control had returned. The horrifying gentleness of his voice warned of anger under so much pressure it must, inevitably, erupt.

"You did not come seeking me," he said. "You believed this was Alpha Ceti VI. Why would you choose to visit a barren world? Why are you here?"

Chekov said nothing.

"Foolish child." As carefully as a father caressing a baby, Khan touched his cheek. His fingers stroked down to Pavel's chin. Then he grabbed his jaw and brutally forced up his head.

Just as suddenly he spun away, grabbed Terrell by the throat, and jerked him off his feet.

"Why?"

Terrell shook his head. Khan gripped harder.

Choking, Terrell clawed at Khan's gloved hand.

Khan watched, a smile on his face, while the captain slowly and painfully lost consciousness.

"It does not please him to answer me," Khan said. His lips curled in a cruelly simple smile. "Well, no matter." He opened his fist, and Terrell's limp body collapsed on the floor.

Chekov twisted, trying to free himself. The two men holding him nearly broke his arms. Chekov gasped. Terrell curled around himself, coughing. But at least he was alive.

"You'll tell me willingly soon enough," Khan said. He made a quick motion with his head. His people dragged Chekov and Terrell into the laboratory and dumped them next to the sand tank.

Khan strode past them, picked up a small strainer, and dipped it into the tank. He lifted it, and sand showered out, sifting down through the mesh and flung up by the struggling of the creatures he had snared.

"Did you, perhaps, come exploring? Then let me introduce you to the only remaining species native to Alpha Ceti V." He thrust the strainer in front of Chekov. "Ceti eels," Khan said. The last of the sand spilled away. The two long, thin eels writhed together, lashing their tails and snapping their narrow pointed jaws. They were the sickly yellow of the sand. They had no eyes. "When our world became desert, only a desert creature could survive." Khan took Chekov's helmet from one of his people, an intense blond young man.

"Thank you, Joachim." He tilted the strainer so one of the eels flopped into the helmet.

Joachim spilled the second eel into Terrell's helmet.

"They killed, they slowly and horribly killed, twenty of my people," Khan said. "One of them . . . was my wife."

"Oh, no. . . ." Chekov whispered. He remembered Lieutenant McGiver. She had been tall and beautiful and classically elegant; but more important, kind and sweet and wise. He had had only one conversation with her, and that by chance—he was an ensign, assigned to the night watch, when she was on the *Enterprise,* and ensigns and officers did not mix much. But once, she had talked with him. For days afterward, he had wished he were older, more experienced, of a more equivalent rank. . . . He had wished many things.

When she left the *Enterprise* to go with Khan, Ensign Pavel Chekov had locked himself in his cabin and cried. How could she go with Khan? He had never understood. He did not understand now.

"You let her die," he said.

Khan's venomous glance transfixed him.

"You may blame her death on your Admiral Kirk," he said. "Do you want to know *how* she died?" He swirled Chekov's helmet in circles. Pavel could hear the eel sliding around inside. "The young eel enters its victim's body, seeks out the brain, and entwines itself around the cerebral cortex. As a side effect, the prey becomes extremely susceptible to suggestion." He came toward Chekov. "The eel grows, my dear Pavel Chekov, within the captive's brain. First it causes madness. Then the host becomes paralyzed—unable to move, unable to feel anything but the twisting of the creature within the skull. I learned the progression well. I watched it happen . . . to my wife."

He lingered over the description, articulating every word with care and precision, as if he were torturing himself, embracing the agony as a fitting punishment.

"Khan!" Pavel cried. "Captain Kirk was only doing his duty! Listen to me, please—"

"Indeed I will, Pavel Chekov: in a few moments you will speak to me as I wish."

Pavel felt himself being pushed forward in a travesty of a bow. He fought, but the guards forced him down. Khan let him look into his helmet, where the eel squirmed furiously.

"Now you must meet my pet, Mr. Chekov. You will find that it is not . . . quite . . . domesticated. . . ."

Khan slammed the helmet over Pavel's head and locked it into its fastenings.

The eel tumbled against Pavel's face, lashing his cheek with its tail. In a panic, he clawed at his faceplate. Khan stood before him, watching, smiling. Pavel grabbed the helmet latches, but Khan's people pulled his hands away and held him still.

The eel, sensing the heat of a living body, ceased its frantic thrashing and began to crawl, probing purposefully with its sharp little snout. Pavel shook his head violently. The eel curled its body through his hair, anchoring itself, and continued its relentless search.

It curved down behind his ear, slid beneath the lobe, and glided up again.

It touched his eardrum.

He heard the rush of blood, and its flowing warmth caressed his cheek.

Then he felt the pain.

He screamed.

On board *Reliant*, Mr. Kyle tried again and again to reach Terrell and Chekov. His voice was tight and strained.

"Reliant to Terrell, *Reliant* to Terrell, come in, Captain. Captain Terrell, please respond."

"For gods' sake, Kyle, stop it," Beach said.

Kyle swung around on him. "Stoney, I can't *find* them," he said. "There's no signal at all!" Several minutes had passed since the cry from Pavel Chekov. The sensor dials trembled in overload.

"I know. Muster a landing party. Full arms. Alert the transporter room. I'm beaming down right now." He headed for the turbo-lift.

*"Terrell to *Reliant*, Terrell to *Reliant*, come in, *Reliant*."*

Beach rushed back to the console.

"Reliant, Beach here. For gods' sake, Clark, are you all right?"

The pause seemed slightly longer than the signal lag required, but Beach dismissed it as his own concern and relief.

"Everything's fine, Commander. I'll explain when I see you. We're bringing several guests aboard. Prepare to beam up on my next signal."

"Guests? Clark, what—?"

"Terrell out."

Beach looked at Kyle, who was frowning.

" 'Guests'?" Kyle said.

"Maybe we *are* transplanting something."

"Enterprise Shuttle Seven, you're cleared for liftoff."

"Roger, Seattle, we copy." Captain Hikaru Sulu powered up the gravity fields, and the square little shuttlecraft rose smoothly from the vast expanse of the landing field.

He glanced around to make sure his passengers were all safely strapped in: Admiral Kirk, Dr. McCoy, Commander Uhura. Almost like the old days. Kirk was reading a book—was that a pair of spectacles he was wearing? It was, indeed—McCoy was making notes in a medical file, and Uhura was bent over a pocket computer, intent on the program she was writing.

Rain the night before had left the day crystal clear and gleaming. The shuttle gave a three-hundred-sixty-degree view of land so beautiful that Hikaru wanted to grab everyone in the shuttle and shake them till they looked: two ranges of mountains, the Cascades to the east and the Olympics to the west, gray and purple and glittering white; the long wide path of Puget Sound, leading north, studded with islands and sliced by the keen-edged wake of a hydrofoil. He rotated the shuttle one hundred eighty degrees to starboard, slowly, facing in turn the solitary volcanic peaks of Mount Baker, Mount Rainier, Mount St. Helens, steaming and smoking again after a two-hundred-year sleep, Mount Hood, and far to the south, rising through towering thunderheads, Mount Shasta.

The shuttle continued its ascent. Distance blurred the evidence of civilization, even of life, stripping the underlying geology bare, until the lithic history of lava flows, glacial advance, and orogeny lay clear before him. A lightning bolt flashed along Mount Shasta's flank, arcing through the clouds.

And then the earth curved away beneath him, disappearing into the sun far to one side and into the great shadow of the terminator on the other.

Uhura reached out and brushed her fingertips against his arm. He glanced around. The computer lay abandoned beside her.

"Thank you," she said very softly. "That was beautiful."

Hikaru smiled, glad to have someone to share it with.

"My pleasure."

She went back to her computer. He homed in on the Starfleet Space Dock beacon and engaged the autopilot. It would be a while before he had anything else to do. He stretched out in one of the passenger seats, where he could relax but still keep an eye on the control display.

The admiral closed his book and pushed his glasses to the top of his head.

"You look a bit the worse for wear, Mr. Sulu—is that from yesterday?"

Hikaru touched the bruise above his cheekbone and grinned ruefully. "Yes, sir. I didn't realize I'd got it till too late to do anything about it."

"There's one thing you can say about Mr. Spock's protégés: They're *always* thorough."

Hikaru laughed. "No matter what they're doing. That was quite a show, wasn't it?"

"It was, indeed. I didn't get much chance to speak to you yesterday. It's good to see you."

"Thank you, sir. The feeling's mutual."

"And by the way, congratulations, Captain."

Hikaru glanced down at the shiny new braid on his uniform. He was not quite used to it yet.

"Thank you, Admiral. You had a lot to do with it. I appreciate the encouragement you've given me all these years."

Kirk shrugged. "You earned it, Captain. And I wasn't the only commander you've had who put in a good word. Spock positively gushed. For Spock, anyway. And you got one of the two or three best recommendations I've ever seen from Hunter."

"I appreciate your letting me know that, Admiral. Both their opinions mean a lot to me."

Kirk glanced around the shuttle. "Almost like old times, isn't it? Do you still keep in touch with your friend Commander Flynn?"

"Yes, sir—I saw her off this morning, in fact. She made captain, early last spring."

"Of course she did; I'd forgotten. When the memory begins to go—" He stopped, then grinned, making it into a joke. But he had sounded terribly serious. "They gave her one of the new ships, didn't they?"

"Yes, sir, *Magellan.* It left today." It will be a long time before I see her again, Hikaru thought with regret.

A long time. The new Galaxy-class ships were smaller than the *Enterprise,* but much faster. They were most efficient around warp twelve. Only three as yet existed: *Andromeda, M-31,* and *Magellanic Clouds.* Their purpose was very long range exploration; commanding such a mission was the career Mandala Flynn, who had been born and raised in space, had aimed for all her life.

Jim Kirk chuckled. Hikaru gave him a questioning glance.

"Do you remember what she said to me at the officers' reception the day she came on board the *Enterprise?*"

"Uh—I'm not sure, sir." Actually he remembered it vividly, but if Admiral Kirk were by chance thinking of something else, Hikaru felt it would be more politic not to remind him of the other.

"I asked her what her plans were, and she looked me straight in the eye and said, 'Captain, I want your job.'"

Hikaru could not repress a smile. Besides remembering that, he also remembered the shocked silence that had followed. Mandala had not meant it as a threat, of course, nor had Kirk taken it as one. Not exactly. But it had not been quite the best foot for a field-promoted officer, a mustang—someone who had worked up from the ranks—to start out on.

"She got it, too," Kirk said softly, gazing out the window and seeing, perhaps, not the earth below or the angular chaos of the space station far ahead, but new worlds and past adventures.

"Sir? Do you mean you put in for a Galaxy ship?" Hikaru felt rather shocked, partly because if Kirk had applied, he must have been turned down, but even more that he had made the request in the first place.

"What? Oh, no. No, of course not. I didn't mean that the way it sounded. She earned her command, just as you did yours. I don't begrudge it to either of you." He grinned. "But if I were ten years younger, she might have had a fight on her hands for one of the Galaxies."

"I can't quite imagine you anywhere but on the bridge of the *Enterprise*, Captain Kirk—uh, sorry—*Admiral*."

"I think I consider that a compliment, Captain Sulu."

The autopilot emitted a soft beep as it engaged the spacedock's guide beacon. Kirk nodded to Sulu, who returned to the controls, deactivated the autopilot, and engaged the navigational computer and communications system.

"Shuttle Seven to *Enterprise*. Admiral Kirk's party on final approach."

"Shuttle Seven, welcome to *Enterprise*. Prepare for docking."

"Thank you, *Enterprise*, we copy."

When Sulu had completed the preparations, Kirk caught his gaze again.

"By the way, Captain, I must thank you for coming along."

"I was delighted to get your request, Admiral. A chance to go back on board the *Enterprise,* to indulge in a bit of nostalgia—how could I pass it up?"

"Yes. . . ." Kirk said thoughtfully. "Nevertheless, I remember how much there was to do, and how little time there seemed to be to do it in, just before I got the *Enterprise.* It's not very long till the end of the month—when you take command of *Excelsior.*"

"I'm ready, sir. I've looked forward to it for a long time."

"I know. I took a lot of pleasure in personally cutting the orders for your first command."

"Thank you, Admiral."

"But I'm still grateful to have you at the helm for three weeks." He grinned: for a moment the somber cloud of responsibility thinned, letting out a flash of Captain James Kirk of the Starship *Enterprise.* He leaned over and said, with mock confidentiality, "Mr. Sulu, I don't believe those kids can steer."

Lieutenant Saavik watched *Enterprise* Shuttle Seven as it settled into its transport moorings; its pilot—Captain Sulu, she assumed—was excellent. The great doors of the starship's landing bay slid closed, and air sighed in to pressurize the compartment.

The other trainees waited nervously for Admiral Kirk. Saavik remained outwardly impassive, though she felt uncomfortable about having to face Kirk after yesterday's disaster. He had merely added to her humiliation by rating her well in the series of simulation exams. She believed he should have significantly downgraded her overall score because of her performance on the final test. She felt confused, and Saavik disliked confusion intensely.

Captain Spock knew far more about humans in

general than Saavik thought she could ever hope to learn, and more about Admiral Kirk in particular. Perhaps he could explain Kirk's motives. Since coming on board, though, Saavik had been too busy to ask him.

"Docking procedures completed," the computer said.

"Prepare for inspection," Spock said. "Open airlock."

All the trainees came to rigid attention as the doors slid open. The computer, surrogate bo'sun, piped the Admiral onto the ship. Kirk paused, saluted the Federation logo before him, and exchanged salutes with Spock.

"Permission to come aboard, Captain?"

"Permission granted, Admiral, and welcome."

Kirk stepped on board the *Enterprise*.

"I believe you know my trainees," Spock said. "Certainly they have come to know you."

Kirk looked straight at Saavik. "Yes," he said, "we've been through death and life together."

Saavik maintained her composure, but only the techniques of biocontrol that Spock had taught her saved her from a furious blush. She could not make out Kirk's tone at all. He might be attempting humor.

For the first ten years of her life, Saavik had never laughed; for the first ten years of her life, she had never seen anyone laugh unless they had caused another person pain.

Humor was not Saavik's forte.

Kirk held her gaze a moment, then, when she did not respond, turned away.

"Hello, Mr. Scott," he said to the chief engineer. "You old spacedog, Scotty, are you well?"

"Aye, Admiral. I had a wee bout, but Dr. McCoy pulled me through."

" 'A wee bout'? A wee bout of what?"

Saavik paid particular attention to the interchange between the humans. Spock said their words were not necessarily significant. Observe their actions toward one another, their expressions. Assign at least as much importance to the tone of voice as to what is said.

The first thing that occurred after the admiral's question was a pause. Inability to answer the question? Saavik dismissed that immediately. Surprise or confusion? Those were possibilities. Reluctance, perhaps?

Mr. Scott glanced at Dr. McCoy—quickly, as if he hoped no one would notice. So: reluctance it was. McCoy returned his look, adding a slight shrug and a small smile.

"Er, shore leave, Admiral," Mr. Scott said.

"Ah," Kirk said.

His tone indicated comprehension, though in fact his question had been not answered, but avoided. Saavik dissected the encounter in her mind and put it back together as best she could. Mr. Scott and Dr. McCoy knew of some event in Mr. Scott's life that the admiral wished to know, but which Mr. Scott would be embarrassed to reveal. Dr. McCoy agreed, by his silence, to conspire in the concealment; the admiral, by his tone of understanding, had appeared to accede to their plan, yet put them both on notice that he intended to find out exactly what had happened, but at some more convenient, perhaps more private, time.

Saavik felt some satisfaction with the intellectual exercise of her analysis; it remained to be seen if it were accurate.

Admiral Kirk strode along before the line, giving each trainee a stern yet not unfriendly glance. Spock and Scott accompanied him.

"And who is this?" Kirk said, stopping in front of the child.

Peter drew himself up so straight and serious that Saavik wanted to smile. He was blond and very fair; under the admiral's inspection his face turned bright pink. He was a sweet child, so enthusiastic he practically glowed, so proud to be in space at fourteen that he lived within a radiating sphere of joy which could not help but affect those around him.

Even Saavik.

Now, undergoing his very first admiral's inspection, Peter replied to Kirk breathlessly. "Cadet First Class Peter Preston, engineer's mate, *sir!*" He saluted stiffly, fast, and with great eagerness.

Kirk smiled, came to attention, and saluted in the same style.

If he laughs at Peter, Saavik thought, I shall certainly rip out his liver.

The civilized part of her, taking over again after the infinitesimal lapse, replied: You most certainly shall not; besides—do you even know where the liver is in a human?

"Is this your first training voyage, Mr. Preston?"

"Yes, *sir!*"

"I see. In that case, I think we should start the inspection with the engine room."

"Aye, sir!"

"I dinna doubt ye'll find all in order," Mr. Scott said.

"We shall see you on the bridge, Admiral," the captain said.

"Very good, Mr. Spock."

Engineer Scott started toward the turbo-lift with Kirk; the engine room company followed. Peter flashed Saavik a quick, delighted grin, and hurried after them.

The rest of the ship's personnel dispersed quickly to attend their posts. Spock and Saavik left for the bridge.

"Have you any observations to make, Lieutenant Saavik?" Spock asked.

"The admiral is . . . not quite what I expected, Captain."

"And what did you expect?"

Saavik paused in thought. What *had* she expected? Spock held James Kirk in high regard, and she had based her preconceptions almost entirely on this fact. I expected him to be like Spock, she thought. But he resembles him not at all.

"He's very . . . human. . . ."

"You must remember that, as a member of Starfleet,

you are unlikely ever to escape the presence of humans, or their influence. Tolerance is essential; in addition, it is logical."

"You are my mentor, Captain. Your instruction has been invaluable to me—indeed, it is indispensable." They stepped into the main turbo-lift.

"Bridge," Spock said. "Saavik, no one exists who has experiences and heritage similar enough to yours to advise you competently. Even I can only tell you that, as a Vulcan and a Romulan in a world of humans, you are forever a stranger. You will have to deal with strangers who may, at times, seem incomprehensible to you."

"Captain," Saavik said carefully, "I confess that I had not expected the admiral to be quite so representative of his culture. However, I intended no prejudice against Admiral Kirk, nor intolerance of human beings."

The doors to the turbo-lift opened onto the bridge, ending the conversation.

Peter Preston stood at attention next to the control console that was his responsibility. It was the second backup system for auxiliary power, and its maintenance records showed that except for testing, it had not even been directly on-line for two years. Nevertheless, Peter had checked out every circuit and every memory nexus and every byte of its data base a dozen times over. Sometimes, late at night when the ship was docked without even a skeleton crew on duty, Peter came down and ran his console through its diagnostic programs. He loved being here all alone in the enormous engine room with the echoes of tremendous energy fluxes scintillating around him.

Peter stood last in line for inspection. He could hardly bear the wait. He knew his console was in perfect shape. But what if Admiral Kirk found something wrong? What if—

The admiral stopped in front of him, looked him up

and down, and drew one finger along the edge of the console. Looking for dust? There definitely was not any dust.

"I believe you'll find everything shipshape, Admiral," Peter said, and immediately wished he had kept his mouth shut.

"Oh, do you?" Kirk said sternly. "Mr. Preston, do you have any idea, any idea at all, how often I've had to listen to Mr. Scott tell me that one more warp factor will blow the ship to bits?"

"Uh, no sir," Peter said, quite startled.

"Mr. Preston, do you know how they refer to the *Enterprise* in the officers' mess?"

"Uh, no sir," Peter said again, and then thought, brilliant line, kid. Why don't you use it one more time and make a *really* good impression?

"Why, they call it 'the flying deathtrap.' And they aren't referring to the food."

"Sir, that's not true! This is the best ship in the whole Starfleet!"

The admiral started to smile, and Mr. Scott chuckled. Peter felt the blood rising to his face. Oh, no, he thought, I fell for it; Dannan warned me, and I *still* fell for it. Dannan, his oldest sister, was already a commander; she was twelve years older than he, and he had absorbed her stories, practically through his skin, since before he could remember. If she saw him now, he knew she would tease him about looking like a ripe tomato, he blushed so hard. That is, if she would even speak to him once she found out he'd acted like such a dope.

"And begging the admiral's pardon, *sir*," Peter said, "but the only person who couldn't see the truth about this ship would have to be as blind as a Tiberian bat! *Sir*."

Kirk looked at him for a moment. Then he reached into his pocket and pulled out a small spidery little construction of glass and gold wire. He unfolded it, balanced it on his nose, hooked some of the wires around his ears, peered closely through the lenses at the console and over the tops of the lenses at the rest of the engine room, and finally turned to Peter again.

"By God, you're right, Mr. Preston. It *is* a good ship."

Dr. McCoy laughed, and so did Mr. Scott. For a horrible moment, Peter was afraid one of the three men was going to reach out and pat him on the head, but they spared him that. As they walked away, he could not help but hear their conversation.

"Scotty, your cadet's a tiger."

"My sister's youngest, Admiral."

Oh, no, Peter thought, why did he have to tell the admiral he's my uncle? Peter himself had told no one in the training group, and he had hoped that Uncle Montgomery hadn't, either. Peter valued his uncle's advice and love and even his occasional crotchetiness, but things would have been easier, clearer somehow, if he were training under someone unrelated to him.

"Crazy to get to space," Mr. Scott said. "Always has been."

"Every youngster's fancy," Admiral Kirk said. "I seem to remember it myself."

They stopped at the far end of the engine room; the admiral listened as Mr. Scott pointed out improvements added since Kirk's last visit.

Peter ducked out of line, sprinted to the tool bay, rummaged around in his bin for a moment, and hurried to his place again.

At the console next to him, Grenni glanced at him sidelong and muttered, "What the hell you doin', Pres? We're not dismissed yet."

"You'll see," Peter whispered.

Kirk and Scott and McCoy strolled back along the length of the engine room. When they reached Peter, the cadet saluted hard.

Kirk stopped. "Yes, Mr. Preston?"

Peter offered him a complicated instrument.

"I believe the admiral asked after this?"

Kirk inspected it.

"What is it, Mr. Preston?"

"Why, sir, it's a left-handed spanner, of course."

Mr. Scott looked completely and utterly shocked. The admiral's mouth twitched. Dr. McCoy choked down a smile, then gave up and started to laugh. After a moment, Kirk followed suit. Mr. Scott managed nothing better than a stiff, grim smile. Peter watched them with his very best total-innocent look.

"Mr. Scott," Kirk said, but he was laughing too hard to continue. Finally he stopped and wiped his eyes. "Mr. Scott, I think we'd better get these kids on their training cruise before they take over completely. Are your engines up to a little trip?"

"Just give the word, Admiral."

"Mr. Scott, the word is given."

"Aye, sir."

Kirk handed the "left-handed spanner" back to Peter and started away. A few steps later, he glanced over his shoulder and winked.

As soon as the turbo-lift doors slid closed, Jim Kirk collapsed into laughter again. "Do you believe it, Bones?" He was laughing so hard he had to pause between every phrase. "God, what a terrific kid. A left-handed spanner!" Jim wiped the tears from his eyes. "I deserved that one, didn't I? I forgot how much I hated being teased when I was his age."

"Yes, once in a while we old goats need to be reminded how things were back in the mists of prehistory."

Kirk's amusement subsided abruptly. He *still* disliked being teased, and McCoy was well aware of the fact. Jim frowned, not knowing how to take McCoy's comment. "Bridge," he said to the turbo-lift voice sensor.

"What about the rest of your inspection . . . Admiral?" McCoy said. He let the tone of his voice creep over into not completely benign mockery. Needling Jim Kirk was one of the few ways to get him to take a good hard look at himself.

Getting him drunk certainly had not worked.

"I'll finish it later, Doctor," Jim said mildly. "After we're under way."

"Jim, do you really think that a three-week training cruise once a year is going to make up for forty-nine other weeks of pushing paper? Do you think it's going to keep you from driving yourself crazy?"

"I thought we got this conversation over with last night," Jim said. "You want to know something? It's getting extremely tedious."

"Yeah, concern from one's friends is a bore, isn't it?"

"Sometimes it is," Jim said. "You're a lot better surgeon than you are a psychotherapist."

The turbo-lift doors opened, and McCoy repressed a curse. A few more minutes and he might have made some kind of breakthrough with Jim.

Or got myself punched in the mouth, he thought. Some breakthrough.

Admiral Kirk stepped out onto the bridge of the *Enterprise,* and Dr. McCoy followed him.

McCoy had to admit it was pleasant to be back. He nodded to Uhura, and she smiled at him. Mr. Sulu had the helm, though just now it appeared that Lieutenant Saavik, first officer and science officer for the training cruise, would be piloting the *Enterprise* for practice. The main difference, of course, was that now Mr. Spock was the captain. He did not relinquish his place to Kirk; to do so would be improper. Heaven forbid that Spock might do anything improper.

"Admiral on the bridge!" Mr. Sulu said.

"As you were," Kirk said before anyone could stand up or salute.

"Starfleet Operations to *Enterprise.* You are cleared for departure."

"Lieutenant Saavik, " Spock said, "clear all moorings."

"Aye, sir."

She set to work. Kirk and McCoy descended to the lower bridge.

"Greetings, Admiral." Spock nodded to McCoy as well. "Dr. McCoy. I trust the inspection went well."

"Yes, Captain, I'm very impressed," Kirk said.

"Moorings clear, Captain," Saavik said.

"Thank you, Lieutenant." Spock paused a moment, and then his eyes got that hooded look that McCoy had learned in self-defense to recognize.

"Lieutenant Saavik," Spock said, "how many times have you piloted a starship out of spacedock?"

"One hundred ninety-three, sir," Saavik said promptly. And then added: "In simulation."

Kirk absolutely froze.

"In real-world circumstances," Saavik said, "never."

McCoy got the distinct impression that Jim Kirk simultaneously thought of two possible courses of action. The first was to pitch Spock out of the captain's seat and order Mr. Sulu to take the helm. The second was to do nothing. He chose the latter. But it was close to a photo finish.

You damned leprechaun! McCoy directed the delighted thought at Spock. Vulcan discipline, indeed!

Deliberately avoiding a look at Kirk, pretending ignorance of the admiral's discomfort, Spock glanced at McCoy with a very slight smile. For the Vulcan, that was almost as extreme a reaction as Jim's fit of laughter in the turbo-lift was for Kirk.

"Take us out, Lieutenant Saavik," Spock said.

"Aye, sir. Reverse thrust, Mr. Sulu, if you please."

"Reverse thrust, Lieutenant."

"It is always rewarding to watch one's students examine the limits of their training," Spock said. "Wouldn't you agree, Admiral?"

"Oh, definitely, Captain. To be sure. First time for everything, after all."

The viewscreen showed the spacedock recede majestically, then spin slowly from their sight as Saavik rotated the *Enterprise* away.

"Ahead one-quarter impulse power, if you please, Captain Sulu," Saavik said.

Jim opened his mouth to speak, took a deep breath and closed his mouth abruptly, and grabbed his hands together behind his back. McCoy leaned toward him.

"Hey, Jim," he whispered, "want a tranquilizer?"

Kirk glared at him and shook his head.

The ship accelerated.

"One-quarter impulse power," Mr. Sulu said; then, a moment later, "Free and clear."

Kirk quietly released the breath he had been holding.

"Course, Captain?" Saavik asked.

Spock turned to Kirk and raised one eyebrow.

"At your discretion, Captain," Kirk said.

Spock got that expression again, and McCoy's suspicion that the Vulcan was as concerned about Kirk as he was intensified.

"Out there, Lieutenant Saavik."

Kirk started.

"Sir?" Saavik glanced back.

"Out there" was something Jim Kirk had said the last time the *Enterprise* was under his command.

"I believe the technical term is 'thataway,' " Spock said.

"Aye, sir," Saavik said, obviously not understanding.

But McCoy could see that Jim understood.

Chapter 4

As soon as the inspection ended, Peter dropped the "left-handed spanner" into its bin and sprinted to his locker. He was late for his math lesson. He scooped up his little computer, banged the locker door closed, turned around, and ran smack into his Uncle Montgomery.

"Uh—" Peter came to attention and saluted. "I'm due in tutorial, sir, with your permission—"

"Permission denied, Cadet. I'll have a few words wi' ye first."

"But, sir, I'll be late!"

"Then ye'll be late! What did ye mean wi' that display of impertinence?"

Oh, boy, Peter thought. Now I'm in for it.

"Sir?" he said innocently, stalling for time.

"Dinna 'sir' me, ye young scoundrel! Were ye trying to embarrass me in front of the admiral? In front of James Kirk himself?"

"You didn't have to tell him who I was!" Peter said. "Nobody knew, till now!"

"Aye, is that so? Ye are embarrassed to be my nephew?"

"You know I'm not! It just seems like everybody will think I only got here because of it."

Montgomery Scott folded his arms across his chest. "Ye have so little faith in ye'sel'?"

"I just want to pull my share," Peter said, and saw that *that* was not the right thing to say, either.

"I see," Uncle Montgomery said. " 'Tis not ye'sel' ye

doesna trust, 'tis me. Ye think I'd do ye the disservice of letting ye off easy? If ye think ye havna been working hard enough, we'll see if we canna gi' ye a bit o' a change."

I'm definitely going to be late to math, Peter thought. Lieutenant Saavik will cancel the lesson, and on top of everything else it's going to take me three days to get uncle over his snit. Well, smart kid, was it worth it?

He remembered the look on the admiral's face when he gave him the "left-handed spanner" and decided that it was.

But not, unfortunately, as far as Uncle Montgomery was concerned.

"You know I don't think that, uncle," Peter said, trying to placate him.

"Ah, *now* it's 'uncle'! And stop changing the subject! Ye havna explained thy behavior!"

"He was testing me, uncle, to see how dumb I am. If that happened, Dannan said—"

"Dannan!" Uncle Montgomery cried. "That sister o' thine has only just missed being thrown in the brig more times than thy computer can count! I'd not take thy sister as a model, mister, if ye know what's good for ye!"

"Wait a minute!" Peter cried. "Dannan is . . . she's—"

It was true she had been disciplined a lot; it was even true that she had nearly been thrown out of Starfleet. But even Uncle Montgomery had told him a million times that once in a while you had to work on your own initiative, and that was what Dannan did. It didn't matter anyway. Dannan was Peter's sister, and he adored her.

"You can't talk about her that way!"

"I'll talk about her any way I please, young mister, and ye shall listen with a civil tongue in thy head."

"Can I go now?" Peter asked sullenly. "I'm already five minutes late, and Lieutenant Saavik won't wait around."

"That's another thing. Ye spend far too much time hanging around after her. D'ye think she's naught to do but endure the attentions of a puppydog?"

"What's *that* supposed to mean?" Peter asked angrily.

"Dinna play the fool wi' thine old uncle, boy. I can see a schoolboy crush—and so can everyone else. My only advice for ye," he said condescendingly, "is dinna wear thy heart on thy sleeve."

"You don't know what you're talking about!"

"Nay? Well, then, be off wi' ye, Mister Know-It-All, if ye are too wise to listen to the advice o' thine elders."

Peter fled from the locker room.

Saavik arrived at tutorial rather late, for the inspection and undocking disarrayed the usual schedule. She was surprised to find that Peter was not there yet, either. Perhaps he had arrived and, not finding Saavik, assumed that the training cruise would change the routine. But she thought he would wait more than two or three minutes. Perhaps Mr. Scott had lectured his trainees after the engine room inspection.

That could take considerable extra time, Saavik thought. I will wait.

When Spock first requested that Saavik tutor Peter Preston in advanced theoretical mathematics, she had prepared herself to decline. Peter, fourteen, was nearly the same age as Saavik had been when the Vulcan research team landed on her birth-world.

Saavik had feared she would compare the charming and well-brought-up young Peter to the creature she had been on Hellguard. She had feared she would resent the advantages childhood had presented to him and withheld from her. She feared her own anger and how she might react if she released it even for a moment.

When she tried to explain all this to the captain, he listened, considerately and with all evidence of understanding. Then he apologized for his own lack of clarity: he had not made a request; he had given an order which he expected Saavik to carry out as a part of her training. Unquestioning obedience was illogical, but trust was essential. If, in all the years that Saavik had known Spock, she had not found him worthy of trust, then she was of course free to refuse the order. Many avenues of training and advancement would still lie open to her. None, however, would permit her to remain under Spock's command.

Spock had been a member of the Vulcan exploratory expedition to Hellguard. He alone forced the other Vulcans to accept their responsibility to the world's abandoned inhabitants, though they had many logical reasons—and unspoken excuses far more involved—for denying any responsibility. Saavik owed her existence as a civilized being, and possibly her life—for people died young and brutally on Hellguard—to Spock's intervention.

She obeyed his order.

Saavik heard Peter running down the hall. He burst in, out of breath and distracted.

"I'm really sorry I'm late," he said. "I came as fast as I could—I didn't think you'd wait."

"I was late, too," she admitted. "I thought perhaps you were delayed by the inspection, as I was." Saavik had to be honest with herself, though: one of the reasons she waited was that she thoroughly enjoyed the time she spent teaching the young cadet. Peter was intelligent and quick, and while their ages were sufficiently different that Peter was still a child and Saavik an adult, they were in fact only six years apart.

"Well . . . sort of."

"Are you prepared to discuss today's lesson?"

"I guess so," he said. "I think I followed projecting the n-dimensional hyperplanes into n-1 dimensional spaces, but I got a little tangled up when they started to intersect."

Saavik interfaced Peter's small computer with the larger monitor.

"Let me look," she said, "and I will try to see where you began . . . getting a little tangled up."

As she glanced through Peter's work, Saavik reflected upon her own extraordinarily erroneous assumption about the way she would react to Peter. Far from resenting the boy, she found great comfort in knowing that her own childhood was anomalous, rather than being the way of a deliberately cruel universe. Cruelty existed, indeed: but natural law did not demand it.

She learned at least as much from Peter as he did from her: lessons about the joy of life and the possibilities for happiness, lessons she could never feel comfortable discussing with Spock, and in fact had avoided even mentioning to him.

But the captain was far more subtle and complex than his Vulcan exterior permitted him to reveal. Perhaps he had not, as she had believed, given her this task to test her control of the anger she so feared. Perhaps she was learning from Peter precisely what Spock had intended.

"Here, Peter," she said. "This is the difficulty." She pointed out the error in one of his equations.

"Huh?"

He looked blankly at the monitor, his mind a thousand light-years from anything.

"Your tangle," she said. "It's right here."

"Oh. Yeah. Okay." He looked at it and blinked, and said nothing.

"Peter, what's wrong?"

"Uh, nothing."

Saavik remained silent for a moment; Peter fidgeted.

"Peter," Saavik said, "you know that I sometimes have difficulty understanding the way human beings react. I need help to learn. If everything is all right, determining why I thought something might be wrong will pose me a serious problem."

"Sometimes there's stuff people don't want to talk about."

"I know—I don't wish to invade your privacy. But if, in truth, you are not troubled, I must revise many criteria in my analyses of behavior."

He took a deep breath. "Yeah, something happened."

"You need not tell me what," Saavik said.

"Can I, if I want?"

"Of course, if you wish."

He hesitated, as if sorting out his thoughts. "Well," he said, "I had this fight with Commander Scott."

"A fight!" Saavik said with considerable distress.

"Not like punching or anything. But that isn't it; he gets snarked off about little stuff all the time."

"Peter, I think it would be better if you did not speak so of your commanding officer."

"Yeah, you're right, only he's been doing it my whole life—his whole life, I guess. I know because he's my uncle."

"Oh," Saavik said.

"I never told anybody on the ship, only now he's started telling people. He told the *admiral*—can you believe it? That's one of the things I got mad about." He stopped and took a deep breath and shook his head. "But . . ."

Saavik waited in silence.

Peter looked up at her, started to blush, and looked away. "He said . . . he said you had better things to do with your time than put up with me hanging around, he said I'm a pest, and he said . . . he said I . . . Never mind. That part's too dumb. He said you probably think I'm a pain."

Saavik frowned. "The first statement is untrue, and the second is ridiculous."

"You mean you don't mind having to give me math lessons?"

"On the contrary, I enjoy it very much."

"You don't think I'm a pest?"

"Indeed, I do not."

"I'm really glad," Peter said. "He thinks I've

been . . . well . . . acting really dumb. He was laughing at me."

"You deserve better than to be laughed at."

He felt humiliated—Saavik could see that. She knew a great deal about humiliation. She would not wish to teach it to another being. She wished she knew a way to ease his pain, but she felt as confused as he did.

"Peter," she said, "I can't resolve your disagreement with your uncle. I can only tell you that when I was a child, I wished for something I could not name. Later I found the name: it was *friend*. I have found people to admire and people to respect. But I never found a friend. Until now."

He looked up at her. "You mean—me?"

"Yes."

Inexplicably, he burst into tears.

Pavel Chekov screamed.

Nothing happened. . . .

His mind and his memory were sharp and clear. He was hyperaware of everything on the bridge of *Reliant:* Joachim beside him at the helm, Terrell sitting blank and trapped at first officer's position, and Khan.

Khan lounged in the captain's seat. The screen framed a full-aft view: Alpha Ceti V dwindled from a globe to a disk to a speck, then vanished from their sight. *Reliant* shifted into warp, and even Alpha Ceti, the star itself, shrank to a point and lost itself in the starfield.

"Steady on course," Joachim said. "All systems normal."

"It was kind of you to bring me a ship so like the *Enterprise,* Mr. Chekov," Khan said.

Fifteen years before, Khan Singh had flipped through the technical data on the *Enterprise;* apparently he had memorized each page with one quick look. As far as Chekov could tell, Khan remembered the information perfectly to this day. With the knowledge, and with Terrell under his control, Khan had little trouble taking over *Reliant*. Most of the crew had worked on unaware that anything was wrong, until Khan's people came upon them, one by one, took them prisoner, and beamed them to the surface of Alpha Ceti V.

The engine room company remained, working in concert with each other, and with eels.

Out of three hundred people, Khan had found only ten troublesome enough to bother killing.

"Mr. Chekov, I have a few questions to ask of you."

Don't answer him, don't answer him.

"Yes."

The questions began.

He answered. He screamed inside his mind; he felt the creature writhing inside his skull; he answered.

Khan questioned Terrell only briefly, but it seemed to give him great pleasure to extract information from Chekov. By the time he finished, he knew each tiny detail of what precious little anyone on *Reliant* had been told about the classified Project Genesis. He knew where they had been, he knew where they were going, and he knew they reported to Dr. Carol Marcus.

"Very good, Mr. Chekov. I'm very pleased with you. But tell me one more thing. Might my old friend Admiral Kirk be involved in your project?"

"No."

"Is he aware of it?"

"I do not know."

With an edge in his voice, Khan asked, "Could he find out about it?"

Kirk was a member of the Fleet General Staff; he had access to any classified information he cared to look up. Chekov tried desperately to keep that knowledge from Khan Singh. His mind was working so fast and well that he *knew*, without any doubt, what Khan planned. He knew it and he feared it.

"Answer me, Mr. Chekov."

"Yes."

Khan chuckled softly, the sound like a caress.

"Joachim, my friend, alter our course. We shall pay a visit to Regulus I."

"My lord—!" Joachim faced his leader, protest in his voice.

"This does not suit your fancy?"

"Khan Singh, I am with you. We all are. But we're free! This is what we've waited for for two hundred years! We have a ship; we can go where we will—"

"I made a promise fifteen years ago, Joachim. You were witness to my oath, then and when I repeated it. Until I keep my word to myself, and to my wife, I am not free."

"Khan, my lord, she never desired revenge."

"You overstep your bounds, Joachim," Khan said dangerously.

The younger man caught his breath, but plunged on. "You escaped the prison James Kirk made for you! You've proved he couldn't hold you, Khan, you've won!"

"He tasks me, Joachim. He tasks me, and I'll have him."

The two men stared at each other; Joachim wavered and turned his head away.

"In fifteen years, this is all I have asked for myself, Joachim," Khan said. "I can have no new life, no new beginning, until I achieve it. I know that you love me, my friend. But if you feel I have no right to any quest, say so. I will free you from the oath you swore to me."

"I'll never break that oath, my lord."

Khan Singh nodded. "Regulus I, Joachim," he said gently.

"Yes, Khan."

"That's it," Carol Marcus said to the main computer. "Genesis eight-two-eight-point-SBR. Final editing. Save it."

"Ok," the computer said.

Carol sighed with disbelief. Finally finished!

"Fatal error," the computer said calmly. "Memory cells full."

"What do you mean, memory full?" She had checked memory space just the day before.

The damned machine began to recite to her the bonehead explanation of peripheral memory. "The memory is full when the size of the file in RAM exceeds—"

"Oh, stop," Carol said.

"Ok."

"Damn! David, I thought you were going to install the Monster's new memory cells!"

All their computers stored information by arranging infinitesimal magnetic bubbles within a matrix held in a bath of liquid hydrogen near absolute zero. The storage was very efficient and very fast and the volume extremely large; yet from the beginning, Genesis had been plagued by insufficient storage. The programs and the data files were so enormous that every new shipment of memory filled up almost as quickly as it got installed. The situation was particularly critical with the Monster, their main computer. It was an order of magnitude faster than any other machine on the station, so of course everyone wanted to use it.

David hurried to her side. "I did," he said. "I had to build a whole new bath for them, but I did it. Are they filled up *already?*"

"That's what it says."

He frowned and glanced around the lab.

"Anybody have anything in storage here they've just been dying to get rid of?"

Jedda, who was a Deltan and prone to quick reactions, strode over with an expression of alarm. "If you delete my quantum data I'll be *most* distressed."

"I don't *want* to delete anything," Carol said, "but I just spent *six weeks* debugging this subroutine, and I've got to have it."

At a lab table nearby, Del March glanced at Vance Madison. Vance grimaced, and Carol caught him at it.

"All right, you guys," Carol said. "Del, have you been using my bubble bath again?"

Del approached, hanging his head; Vance followed, walking with his easy slouch. They're like a couple of kids, Carol thought. *Like* kids? They *are* kids. They were only a few years older than David.

"Geez, Carol," Del said, "it's just a little something—"

"Del, there's got to be ninety-three computers on Spacelab. Why do you have to put your games on the main machine?"

"They work a lot better," Vance said in his soft, beautiful voice.

"You can't play Boojum Hunt on anything less, Carol," Del said. "Hey, you ought to look at what we did to it. It's got a black hole with an accretion disk that will jump right out and grab you, and the graphics are fantastic. If I do say so myself. If we had a three-d display . . ."

"Why do I put up with this?" Carol groaned. The answer to that was obvious: Vance Madison and Del March were the two sharpest quark chemists in the field, and when they worked together their talents did not simply add, but multiplied. Every time they published a paper, they got another load of invitations to scientific conferences. Genesis was lucky to have them, and Carol knew it.

The two young scientists played together as well as they worked; unfortunately, what they liked to play was computer games. Del had tried to get her to play one once; she was not merely uninterested, she was totally disinterested.

"What's the file name?" she asked. She felt too tired for patience. She turned back to the console. "Prepare to kill a file," she said to the computer.

"Ok," it replied.

"Don't kill it, Carol," Del said. "Come on, give us a break."

She almost killed it anyway; Del's flakiness got to her worst when she was exhausted.

"We'll keep it out of your hair from now on, Carol," Vance said. "I promise."

Vance never said anything he did not mean. Carol relented.

"Oh—all right. What's the file name?"

"BH," Del said.

"Got one in there called BS, too?" David asked.

Del grinned sheepishly. Carol accessed one of the smaller lab computers.

"Uh, Carol," Del said, "I don't think it'll fit in that one."

"How big *is* it?"

"Well . . . about fifty megs."

"Christ on a crutch!" David said. "The program that swallowed Saturn."

"We added a lot since you played it last," Del said defensively.

"Me? I never play computer games!"

Vance chuckled. David colored. Carol hunted around for enough peripheral storage space and transferred the program.

"All right, twins," she said. She liked to tease them by calling them twins: Vance was two meters tall, slender, black, intense, and calm, while Del was almost thirty centimeters shorter, compact, fair, manic, and quick-tempered.

"Thanks, Carol," Vance said. He smiled.

Jedda folded his arms. "I trust this means my data is safe for another day."

"Safe and sound."

The deepspace communicator signaled, and he went to answer it.

Carol stored the Genesis subroutine again.

"Ok," the computer said; and a moment later, "Command?"

Carol breathed a sigh of relief. "Load Genesis, complete."

A moment's pause.

"Ok."

"And run it."

"Ok."

"Now," Carol said, "we wait."

"Carol," Jedda said at the communicator, "it's *Reliant.*"

She got up quickly. Everyone followed her to the communicator. Jedda put the call up on the screen.

"*Reliant* to Spacelab, come in Spacelab."

"Spacelab here, Commander Chekov. Go ahead."

"Dr. Marcus, good. We're en route to Regulus. Our ETA is three days from now."

"Three days? Why so soon? What did you find on Alpha Ceti VI?"

Chekov stared into the screen. What's wrong? Carol wondered. There shouldn't be any time lag on the hyper channel.

"Has something happened? Pavel, do you read me? Has something happened?"

"No, nothing, Doctor. All went well. Alpha Ceti VI checked out."

"Break out the beer!" Del said.

"But what about—"

Chekov cut her off. "We have new orders, Doctor. Upon our arrival at Spacelab, we will take all Project Genesis materials into military custody."

"Bullshit!" David said.

"Shh, David," Carol said automatically. "Commander Chekov, this is extremely irregular. Who gave this order?"

"Starfleet Command, Dr. Marcus. Direct from the General Staff."

"This is a civilian project! This is *my* project—"

"I have my orders."

"What gold-stripe lamebrain gave the order?" David shouted.

Chekov glanced away from the screen, then turned back.

"Admiral James T. Kirk."

Carol felt the blood drain from her face.

David pushed past her toward the screen.

"I knew you'd try to pull this!" he shouted. "Anything anybody does, you just can't wait to get your hands on it and kill people with it!" He reached to cut off the communication.

Carol grabbed his hand. Keep hold of yourself, she thought, and took a deep breath.

"Commander Chekov, the order is improper. I'll permit no military personnel access to my work."

Chekov paused again, glanced away again.

What's going on out there? Carol thought.

"I'm sorry you feel that way, Dr. Marcus," Chekov said. "The orders are confirmed. Please be prepared to hand over Genesis upon our arrival in three days. *Reliant* out."

He reached forward; the transmission faded.

On Spacelab, everyone started talking at once.

"Will everybody please *shut up!*" Carol said. "I can't even think!"

The babble slowly subsided.

"It's got to be a mistake," Carol said.

"A mistake! Mother, for gods' sake! It's perfect! They came sucking up to us with a ship. 'At our disposal!' Ha!"

"Waiting to dispose of us looks more like it," Jedda said.

"David—"

"And what better way to keep an eye on what we're doing? All they had to do was wait till practically everybody is on leave; they can swoop in here and there's only us to oppose them!"

"But—"

"They think we're a bunch of pawns!"

"David, stop it! You're always accusing the military of raving paranoia. What do you think *you're* working up to? Starfleet's kept the peace for a hundred years. . . ."

Silence fell. David could not deny what she had said. At the same time, Carol could not explain what had happened.

"Mistake or not," Vance said, "if they get Genesis, they aren't likely to give it back."

"You're right," Carol said. She thought for a moment. "All right, everybody. Get your gear together. Start with lab notes and work down from there. Jedda, is Zinaida asleep?" Carol knew that Zinaida, Genesis's mathematician, had been working on the dispersal equations until early that morning.

"She was when I left our room," he said. Like Jedda, Zinaida was a Deltan. Deltans tended to work and travel in groups, or at the very least in pairs, for a Deltan alone was terribly isolated. They required emotional and physical closeness of such intensity that no other sentient being could long survive intimacy with one of them.

"Okay, you'd better wake her. Vance, Del, Misters Computer Wizards: I want you to start transferring everything in the computers to portable storage, because any program, any data we can't move we're going to kill—that goes for BH or BS or whatever it is, too. So get to work."

"But where are we going?" Del asked.

"That's for us to know and *Reliant* to find out. But we've only got three days. Let's not waste time."

The doors of the turbo-lift began to close.

"Hold, please!"

"Hold!" Jim Kirk said to the sensors. The doors opened obediently, sighing.

Lieutenant Saavik dashed inside.

"Thank you, sir."

"My pleasure, Lieutenant."

She gazed at him intently; Kirk began to feel uneasy.

"Admiral," she said suddenly, "may I speak?"

"Lieutenant," Kirk said, "self-expression does not seem to be one of your problems."

"I beg your pardon, sir?"

"Never mind. What was it you wanted to say?"

"I wish to ask you about the high efficiency rating."

"You earned it."

"I did not think so."

"Because of the results of *Kobayashi Maru?*"

"I failed to resolve the situation," Saavik said.

"You couldn't. There isn't any resolution. It's a test of character."

She considered that for a moment.

"Was the test a part of your training, Admiral?"

"It certainly was," Jim Kirk said with a smile.

"May I ask how *you* dealt with it?"

"You may ask, Lieutenant." Kirk laughed.

She froze.

"That was a little joke, Lieutenant," Kirk said.

"Admiral," she said carefully, "the jokes human beings make differ considerably from those with which I am familiar."

"What jokes exactly do you mean?"

"The jokes of Romulans," she said.

Do you want to know? Jim Kirk asked himself. You don't want to know.

"Your concept, Admiral," Saavik said, "the human concept, appears more complex and more difficult."

Out of the blue, he thought, My *God*, she's beautiful.

Watch it, he thought; and then, sarcastically, You're an *admiral*.

"Well, Lieutenant, we learn by doing."

She did not react to that, either. He decided to change the subject.

"Lieutenant, do you want my advice?"

"Yes," she said in an odd tone of voice.

"You're allowed to take the test more than once. If you're dissatisfied with your performance, you should take it again."

The lift slowed and stopped. The doors slid open and

Dr. McCoy, who had been waiting impatiently, stepped inside.

All this newfangled rebuilding, he thought, and look what comes of it: everything's even slower.

"Who's been holding up the damned elevator?— Oh!" he said when he saw Kirk and Saavik. "Hi."

"Thank you, Admiral," Saavik said as she stepped off the lift. "I appreciate your advice. Good day, Doctor."

The doors closed.

Jim said nothing but stared abstractedly at the ceiling.

Doing his very best dirty old man imitation, McCoy waggled his eyebrows.

"Did she change her hair?"

"What?"

"I said—"

"I heard you, Bones. Grow up, why don't you?"

Well, McCoy thought, *that's* a change. Maybe not a change for the better, but at least a change.

"Wonderful stuff, that Romulan ale," McCoy said with a touch of sarcasm.

Kirk returned from his abstraction. "It's a great memory restorative," he said.

"Oh—?"

"It made me remember why I never drink it."

"That's gratitude for you—"

"Admiral Kirk," Uhura said over the intercom. "Urgent message for Admiral Kirk."

Jim turned on the intercom. "Kirk here."

"Sir, Regulus I Spacelab is on the hyperspace channel. Urgent. Dr. Carol Marcus."

Jim started.

Carol Marcus? McCoy thought. *Carol Marcus?*

"Uh . . . Uhura, I'll take it in my quarters," Jim said.

"Yes, sir."

He turned the intercom off again and glared at

McCoy, as if having any witnesses to his reaction irritated him.

"Well, well, well," McCoy said. "It never rains but it—"

"Some doctor you are," Jim said angrily. "You of all people should appreciate the danger of opening old wounds."

The lift doors opened, and Kirk stormed out.

"*Sor*ry," McCoy said after the doors had closed once more. Well, Old Family Doctor, he thought, needling him isn't working; you'd better change your tack if you want to bring him out of his funk.

On the other hand, McCoy said to himself, depending on what that call is about, you may not have to.

Jim Kirk strode down the corridor of the *Enterprise,* trying to maintain his composure. Carol Marcus, after all these years? It would have to be something damned serious for her to call him. And what, in heaven's name, was going on with McCoy? Every word the doctor had said in the past three days was like a porcupine, layered over with little painful probes veiled and unveiled.

He hurried into his room and turned on the viewscreen.

"Dr. Marcus, Admiral," Uhura said.

The image snowed and fluttered across the viewscreen. For an instant, he could make out Carol's face; then it fragmented again.

"Uhura, can't you augment the signal?"

"I'm trying, sir, it's coming in badly scrambled."

". . . Jim . . . read me? Can you . . ."

What did come through clearly was Carol Marcus's distress and anger.

"Your message is breaking up, Carol. What's the matter? What's wrong?"

". . . can't read you. . . ."

"Carol, what's wrong?" He kept repeating that,

hoping enough would get through for her to make out his question.

". . . trying . . . take Genesis away from us. . . ."

"What?" he asked, startled. "Taking Genesis? Who? Who's taking Genesis?"

". . . can't hear you. . . . Did you order . . . ?"

"What order? Carol, *who's taking Genesis?*"

The transmission cleared for a mere few seconds. "Jim, rescind the order." It began to break up again. ". . . no authority . . . I won't let . . ."

"Carol!"

"Jim, please help. I don't believe—"

The picture scrambled again and did not clear. Jim slammed his hand against the edge of the screen.

"Uhura, what's happening? Damn it!"

"I'm sorry, sir. There's nothing coming through. It's jammed at the source."

"Jammed!"

"That's what the pattern indicates, Admiral."

"Damn," Jim said again. "Commander, alert Starfleet HQ. I want to talk to Starfleet Command."

"Aye, sir."

Jim Kirk strode onto the bridge.

"Mr. Sulu," he said, "stop impulse engines."

Sulu complied. "Stop engines."

The bridge crew waited, surprised, expectant, confused.

"We have an emergency," Kirk said stiffly. "By order of Starfleet Command, I am assuming temporary command of the *Enterprise.* Duty Officer, so note in the ship's log. Mr. Sulu, plot a new course: Regulus I Spacelab." He paused as if waiting for an objection or an argument. No one spoke. He opened an intercom channel to the engine room. "Mr. Scott."

"Aye, sir?"

"We'll be going to warp speed immediately."

"Aye, sir."

"Course plotted for Spacelab, Admiral," Mr. Sulu said.

"Engage warp engines."

"Prepare for warp speed," Saavik said. Her voice was tense and suspicious; only the regard in which Captain Spock held this human kept her from rebelling. She shifted the ship to warp mode.

"Ready, sir," said Mr. Sulu.

"Warp five, Mr. Sulu."

The ship gathered itself around them and sprang.

Kirk stepped back into the turbo-lift and disappeared.

In his cabin, Spock lay on a polished slab of Vulcan granite, his meditation stone. He was preparing himself to sink from light trance to a deeper one when he felt the *Enterprise* accelerate to warp speed. He immediately brought himself back toward consciousness. A moment later, he heard someone at his door.

"Come," he said quietly. He sat up.

Jim Kirk entered, hitched one hip on the corner of the stone, and stared at the floor.

"Spock, we've got a problem."

Spock arched his eyebrow.

"Something's happened at Regulus I. We've been ordered to investigate."

"A difficulty at the Spacelab?"

"It looks like it." He raised his head. "Spock, I told Starfleet all we have is a boatload of children. But we're the only ship free in the octant. If something *is* wrong . . . Spock, your cadets—how good *are* they? What happens when the pressure is real?"

"They are living beings, Admiral; all living beings have their own gifts." He paused. "The ship, of course, is yours."

"Spock . . . I already diverted the *Enterprise*. Haste seemed essential at the time. . . ."

"The time to which you are referring, I assume, is

two minutes and thirteen seconds ago, when the ship entered warp speed?"

Kirk grinned sheepishly. "I should have come here first, I know—"

"Admiral, I repeat: The ship is yours. I am a teacher. This is no longer a training cruise, but a mission. It is only logical for the senior officer to assume command."

"But it may be nothing. The transmission was pretty garbled. If you—as captain—can just take me to Regulus—"

"You are proceeding on a false assumption. I am a Vulcan. I have no ego to bruise."

Jim Kirk glanced at him quizzically. "And now you're going to tell me that logic alone dictates your actions."

"Is it necessary to remind you of something you know well?" He paused. "Logic does reveal, however, that you erred in accepting promotion. You are what you were: a starship commander. Anything else is a waste."

Kirk grinned. "I wouldn't presume to debate you."

"That is wise." Spock stood up. "In any case, were the circumstances otherwise, logic would still dictate that the needs of the many outweigh the needs of the few."

"Or the one?"

"Admiral—" Spock said. He stopped, then began again. "Jim, you are my superior officer. But you are also my friend. I have been, and remain, yours. I am offering you the truth as I perceive it, for myself and for you."

"Spock—" Kirk said quietly. He reached out.

Spock drew back within himself.

Kirk respected the change. He let his hand fall.

"Will you come to the bridge? I didn't do much explaining, and I think your students wonder if I've mutinied."

"Yes, Admiral. But perhaps we'd best talk with Mr.

Scott first, so he may explain the situation to his cadets as well."

That day at lunchtime, Saavik went to the cafeteria and got in line. All around her, her classmates speculated about the change in plan, the *Enterprise*'s new course, the admiral's unusual move in taking over the ship. Saavik, too, wondered what all these abrupt changes meant. She leaned toward the view that it was another, more sophisticated, training simulation.

A few minutes after the admiral's order, Captain Spock had returned to the bridge accompanying Admiral Kirk. He assured the crew that Kirk's action had his consent. Yet Saavik still felt uncomfortable about the whole procedure.

She hesitated over her choice of lunch. She would have preferred steak tartare, but the captain considered eating meat—raw meat in particular—an uncivilized practice at best; consequently Saavik ordinarily chose something else when she was to take a meal in his company. She had tried for a long time to conform to the Vulcan ideal, vegetarianism, but had succeeded only in making herself thoroughly sick.

She compromised, choosing an egg dish which came out of the galley in a profoundly bland state, but which could be made nearly palatable by the addition of a large amount of sesame oil and pippali, a fiery spice. Peter Preston had taken a taste of it once, and Saavik had not warned him to use it sparingly. She had had no idea of the effect it would have on a human being. Once he stopped coughing and drinking water and could talk again, he described it as "a sort of combination of distilled chili and nuclear fission."

She wondered where Peter was. They occasionally ate together; but though now was his lunch break, he was not in the cafeteria.

Saavik stopped beside Captain Spock's table. He was eating a salad.

"May I join you, sir?"

"Certainly, Lieutenant."

She sat down and tried to think of a proper way to voice her concern about the admiral's having taken command of the *Enterprise*.

"Lieutenant," Spock said, "how are Mr. Preston's lessons proceeding?"

"Why—very well, sir. He's an excellent student and has a true aptitude for the subject."

"I thought perhaps he might be finding the work too difficult."

"I've seen no evidence of that, Captain."

"Yet Mr. Scott has asked me to suspend Mr. Preston's tutorial."

"Why?" Saavik asked, startled.

"His explanation was that the engines require work, and that Preston's help is needed."

"The engines," Saavik said, "just scored one hundred fifteen percent on the postoverhaul testing."

"Precisely," Spock said. "I have considered other explanations. An attempt by Mr. Scott to shield Preston from overwork seemed a possibility."

Saavik shook her head. "First, Captain, I believe Peter feels comfortable enough around me that he would let me know if he felt snowed under—"

" 'Snowed under'?"

"Severely overworked. I beg your pardon. I did not intend to be imprecise."

"I meant no criticism, Lieutenant—your progress in dealing with human beings can only be improved by learning their idioms."

Saavik compared Scott's odd request to her earlier conversation with Peter. "I believe I know why Mr. Scott canceled Cadet Preston's tutorial."

She explained what had happened.

Spock considered. "The action seems somewhat extreme. Mr. Scott surely realizes that proper training is worth all manner of inconvenience—for student and teacher. Did Mr. Preston say anything else?"

"He preferred not to repeat part of it. He said it was . . . 'too dumb.' He seemed embarrassed."

"Indeed." Spock ate a few bites of his salad; Saavik tasted her lunch. She added more pippali.

"Saavik," Spock said, "has the cadet shown any signs of serious attachment to you?"

"What do you mean, sir?"

"Does he express affection toward you?"

"I suppose one might say that, Captain. He appeared quite relieved when I told him that I do not consider him a 'pest.' And I must confess . . ." she said, somewhat reluctantly, "I am . . . rather fond of him. He's a sweet-natured and conscientious child."

"But he is," Spock said carefully, "a child."

"Of course." Saavik wondered what Spock was leading up to.

"Perhaps Mr. Scott is afraid his nephew is falling in love with you."

"That's ridiculous!" Saavik said. "Even were it not highly improper, it would be impossible."

"It *would* be improper. But not impossible, or even unlikely. It is, rather, a flaw of human nature. If Cadet Preston develops what humans call a 'crush' on you—"

"Sir?" Now she felt confused.

"A crush, for humans, is something like falling in love; however, it occurs only in very young members of the species and is looked upon with great amusement by older members."

The reasons for Peter's behavior suddenly became much clearer. If this were what he was too embarrassed to tell her about, no wonder. She was well aware how much he disliked being laughed at.

Spock continued. "You must deal with it as best you can, as gently as you can. Human beings are very vulnerable in these matters, and very easily hurt. And, as you quite correctly pointed out, it would be improper—"

Saavik felt both shocked and uncomfortable. "Mr. Spock," she said, returning to the title she had used for him for many years, "Peter is a *child*. And even if falling in love is a flaw of human nature, it is not one of Vulcan nature."

"But you are not a Vulcan," Spock said.

Saavik dropped her fork clattering onto her plate and stood up so fast that her chair rattled across the floor.

"Sit down," Spock said gently.

Unwillingly, she obeyed.

"Saavik, do not misunderstand me. Your behavior as regards Cadet Preston is completely proper—I entertain no doubts of that. I am not concerned with him for the moment, but with you."

"I've tried to learn Vulcan ways," she said. "If you will tell me where I've failed—"

"Nor are we speaking of failure."

"I—I don't understand."

"I chose the Vulcan path when I was very young. For many years, I considered it the best, indeed the only, possible choice for any reasoning being. But . . ." He stopped for a moment, then appeared to change the subject. "I spoke to you of tolerance and understanding—"

Saavik nodded.

"I have come to realize that what is proper for one being may not be correct for another. In fact, it may be destructive. The choice is more difficult for someone with two cultures—"

"I have only one!"

"—who must choose between them, or choose to follow another's lead, or choose a path that is unique. You are unique, Saavik."

"Mr. Spock, what does this have to do with Peter Preston?"

"It has nothing at all to do with Mr. Preston."

"Then what are you trying to say to me?"

"What I am trying to say—and I am perhaps not the most competent person to say it, but there is no other—is that some of the decisions you make about your life may differ from what I might decide, or even from what I might advise. You should be prepared for this possibility, so that you do not reject it when it appears. Do you understand?"

She was about to tell him that she did not, but she felt sufficiently disturbed and uneasy—as, to her surprise, Mr. Spock appeared to feel also—that she wanted to end the conversation.

"I'd like to think about what you've said, Captain." Saavik put herself, and Spock, back into their relationship of subordinate and commander.

"Very good, Lieutenant," he said, acquiescing to the change.

She stood up. "I must get back to the bridge, sir."

"Dismissed, Lieutenant."

She started to go, then turned back. "Sir—what about Cadet Preston's tutorial?"

Spock folded his hands and considered the question. "It must resume, of course. However, Mr. Scott has made a statement about the condition of the engine room which would be indelicate to challenge. I will wait a day or two, then suggest that the lessons continue. Do you find that agreeable?"

"Yes, sir. Thank you."

Saavik returned to her post. She had a great deal to think about.

Chapter 5

Peter Preston stood stiffly at attention. His shoulders ached. He had been there close to an hour, waiting for Commander Scott to inspect—for the third time today —the calibration of Peter's control console.

This is getting old real fast, Peter thought.

His uncle had not cracked a smile or spoken to him in anything but a completely impersonal tone for two days. He was showing considerable displeasure in work that before the training cruise—and before their disagreement—he had unstintingly approved. Just now he was unsatisfied with Peter's maintenance of the console.

Finally the engineer strode over and stopped in front of him.

"Ye ha' stood here a considerable while, Cadet. Are ye so sure this is fixed that ye can afford to waste time lounging?"

"The console was ready at eleven hundred hours, as you ordered, sir."

"So, ye think *this time* ye ha' it working properly, do ye?"

"Aye, sir."

"We'll see abou' that."

Commander Scott ran it through a diagnostic or two.

"Nay," he said, "now ye ha' a field imbalance; ye've overcompensated. Calibrate it again, Cadet."

In a hesitation of a fraction of a second, Peter thought: Dannan said there are times when you have to stick up for yourself, but there are times when you have to prove you can take whatever they can dish out."

"Aye, sir," Peter said, "Sorry, sir."

"As well ye' might be. *Will* ye try to do it right?"

"Aye, sir."

This is definitely one of those times when you have to prove you can take it, Peter thought.

And I *can* take it, too.

He set to work on the console again.

He was still at it when the trainees came back from lunch. Grenni sat down at his station.

"Hey, Pres," he said out of the side of his mouth, "the Old Man's really got it in for you today, doesn't he?"

"Why're you talking like you're in an old prison movie?" Peter said. "He's not going to put you on bread and water just for talking to me."

"You never know."

Peter snorted.

"I told you you shouldn't have pulled that dumb stunt with the admiral," Grenni said.

"Yeah, and I guess you'll keep on telling me, huh?" Peter said. Grenni had all the self-righteousness of twenty-twenty hindsight. That was getting as old as Uncle Montgomery's bad humor.

"Geez, Pres, you're working so hard it makes me tired just to watch you," Grenni said.

"Don't worry," Peter told him. "You won't have to endure the torture much longer. Commander Scott's tantrums never last more than three days. Or hadn't you noticed?"

"No," Grenni said, "I hadn't noticed. But then I haven't had the opportunity to observe him like some people—not being his nephew and all."

Damn, Peter thought. Grenni heard, and that means even if nobody else did, they all know now. *Damn*.

"*Enterprise* to Regulus I Spacelab, come in, Spacelab. Dr. Marcus, please respond."

Uhura's transmissions met with no reply.

She glanced up at Spock.

"It's no use. There's just nothing there."

"But the transmissions are no longer jammed?"

"No, there's no jamming—no nothing."

Spock turned to Kirk, back in his old familiar place on the bridge.

"There are two possibilities, Admiral," Spock said. "That they are unwilling to respond, or that they are unable to respond."

"How long—?"

"We will reach Spacelab in twelve hours and forty-three minutes at our present speed."

Kirk folded his arms and hunched down in the captain's chair. "'Give up Genesis,' she said. What in God's name does that mean? Give it up to whom?"

"It might help my analysis if I knew what Genesis was," Spock said.

Kirk wrestled with conflicting duties, conflicting necessities.

"You're right," he said finally. "Something's happened—something serious. It would be dangerous not to tell you." He stood up. "Uhura, please ask Dr. McCoy to join us in my quarters. Lieutenant Saavik, you have the conn."

The three officers gathered in Jim Kirk's cabin. Spock and McCoy waited while Kirk proved himself to the highest security safeguards.

"Computer," he said. "Security procedure: access to Project Genesis summary."

"Identify for retinal scan," the computer replied.

"Admiral James T. Kirk, Starfleet General Staff. Security Class One."

An instant's pulse of bright light recorded his eyes' patterns; then the screen blinked in filtered colors as the computer ran its comparison programs.

"Security clearance Class One: granted."

"Summary, please," Kirk said.

The computer flashed messages to itself across its screen for several more seconds, until finally an approval overlay masked the safeguards and encodings.

The summary tape began. Carol Marcus, in her lab, faced the camera.

Kirk recognized her son at the next table. David resembled his mother strongly: slender, with high cheekbones, very fair. His curly hair was more gold, while Carol's was ash blond, but they had the same eyes.

Jim had met David Marcus once, years ago, by chance. He recalled the encounter with no particular pleasure. Though David Marcus did not seem to have anything personal against Jim Kirk—for which Jim was grateful if only for the sake of his memories of Carol— the young scientist clearly had little use for military personnel.

Carol faced the camera like an adversary and began to speak.

"I'm Dr. Carol Marcus, director of the Project Genesis team at Regulus I Spacelab. Genesis is a procedure by which the molecular structure of matter is broken down, not into subatomic parts as in nuclear fission, or even into elementary particles, but into sub-elementary particle-waves. These can then, by manipulation of the various nuclear forces, be restructured into anything else of similar mass."

"Fascinating," Spock said.

"Wait," said Kirk.

"Stage one of the experiment has been completed here in the lab. We will attempt stage two underground. Stage three involves the process on a planetary scale, as projected by the following computer simulation."

The tape switched to the sharp-edged ultrarealistic scenes of computer graphics.

"We intend to introduce the Genesis device via torpedo into an astronomical body of Earth's mass or smaller."

A gray barren, cratered world appeared on the screen.

"The planet will be scrupulously researched to preclude the disruption of any life forms or pre-biotics."

Jim, who had already seen the tape, watched the reactions of Spock and McCoy. Relaxed and intent, Spock took in the information. McCoy sat on the edge of his chair, leaning forward, scowling as the images progressed before him.

"When the torpedo impacts the chosen target," Carol said, "the Genesis effect begins."

On the screen, the planet quivered; then, just perceptibly, it expanded. For an instant, it glowed as intensely as a star.

"The Genesis wave dissociates matter into a homogenous mass of real and virtual sub-elementary particles."

The forces of gravity and rotation warred, until it became clear that no structure remained to the planet at all.

"The sub-elementaries reaggregate instantaneously."

An entire world had become a translucent cloud. The mass spread into a disk and almost as quickly coalesced again, reenacting planetary evolution at a billion times the speed.

"Precisely *what* they reform into depends on the complexity of the quantum resonances of the original Genesis wave, and on the available mass. If sufficient matter is present, the programming permits an entire star system to be formed. The simulation, however, deals only with the reorganization of a planetary body."

The sphere solidified, transformed into a new world of continents, islands, oceans. Clouds misted the globe in pinwheel weather patterns.

"In other words," Carol said, "the results are completely under our control. In this simulation, a barren rock becomes a world with water, atmosphere, and a functioning ecosystem capable of sustaining most known forms of carbon-based life."

Wherever the clouds thinned, they revealed a tinge of green.

"It represents only a fraction of the potential that Genesis offers, if these experiments are pursued to their conclusion."

An eerily Earth-like world revolved silently before them on the screen.

"When we consider the problems of population and food supply, the value of the process becomes clear. In addition, it removes the technical difficulties and the ethical problems of interfering with a natural evolutionary system in order to serve the needs of the inhabitants of a separate evolutionary system."

Carol Marcus returned to the screen.

"This concludes the demonstration tape. I and my colleagues, Jedda Adzhin-Dall, Vance Madison, Delwin March, Zinaida Chitirih-Ra-Payjh, and David Marcus, thank you for your attention."

The tape ended.

"It literally *is* genesis," Spock said.

"The power," Kirk said, "of creation."

"Have they proceeded with their experiments?"

"Carol made the tape a year ago. The team got the Federation grant they were applying for, so I assume they've reached phase two by now."

"Dear Lord . . ." McCoy said. He looked up, stricken. "Are we—can we control this? Suppose it hadn't been a lifeless satellite? Suppose that thing were used on an inhabited world?"

"It would," Spock said, "destroy all life in favor of its new matrix."

"Its 'new matrix'? Spock, have you any idea what you're saying?"

"I was not attempting to evaluate its ethical implications, Doctor."

"The ethical implications of complete destruction!"

Spock regarded him quizzically. "You forget, Dr.

McCoy, that sentient beings have had, and used, weapons of complete destruction for thousands of years. Historically it has always been easier to destroy than to create."

"Not anymore!" McCoy cried. "Now you can do both at once! One of our myths said Earth was created in six days; now, watch out! Here comes Genesis! We'll do it for you in six minutes!"

"Any form of power, in the wrong hands—"

"Whose are the right hands, my cold-blooded friend? Are you in favor of these experiments?"

"Gentlemen—" Kirk said.

"Really, Dr. McCoy, you cannot ban knowledge because you distrust its implications. Civilization can be considered an attempt to control new knowledge for the common good. The intent of this experiment is creation, not destruction. Logic—"

"Don't give me logic! My God! A force that destroys, yet leaves what was destroyed still usable? Spock, that's the most attractive weapon imaginable. We're talking about Armageddon! Complete, universal, *candy-coated* Armageddon!"

"Knock it off!" Kirk said. "Both of you. Genesis is already here, Spock; you don't need to argue for its existence."

McCoy started to speak, but Kirk swung around and silenced him with a look.

"Bones, you don't need to argue how dangerous it might be if it falls into the wrong hands. We know that. And it may already have happened. I need you both— and not at each other's throats."

Spock and McCoy looked at each other.

"Truce, Doctor?" Spock said.

Grudgingly, McCoy replied, "Truce." Then he added, "Besides, that was a simulation. The whole idea's preposterous—it probably won't even work in real life."

"On the contrary, the probability of success appears extremely high."

"And how would you know, Spock? You haven't known about it any longer than I have."

"That is true. But Marcus is an excellent scientist, and her research team carries impressive credentials."

"Do you know them, Spock?" Kirk asked.

"Adzhin-Dall is a quantum physicist, and Chitirih-Ra-Payjh is a mathematician. Neither is well known, because their work is not translatable from the original Deltan. But the work itself contains fascinating implications. As for Madison and March, I encountered them some two years ago at a symposium they attended immediately after attaining their doctoral degrees." He spoke rather dryly, because their presentation had been, to say the least, unique.

A decade before, Jaine and Nervek had done the theoretical work in "kindergarten physics"—so-called because it dealt with sub-elementary particles. Madison and March experimentally validated the theory. Their first breakthrough was the dissolution of elementary particles into sub-elementary particles.

Quarks have fractional charge of one-third or two-thirds, and attributes such as charm and strangeness. The sub-elementary particles had fractional charge as well: four-ninths and one-ninth, the squares of the charges of the quark. According to Madison, they could be sorted further by "five unmistakable marks," which the team had proposed designating taste, tardiness, humor, cleanliness, and ambition.

All this had begun to sound peculiarly familiar to Spock. He searched his memory for resonances. Just as he finally came upon the proper reference, March took over to offer terminology for the particles themselves.

When March recited several stanzas of a poem by a Terran nonsense writer, half the audience had responded with delighted laughter, and the other half with offended silence.

Spock had maintained his reserve, but in truth he had been very tempted to smile.

"We'd like to propose that the sub-elementary particles be designated *snarks* and *boojums,*" March had said. "When we picked the names, we didn't realize quite how appropriate they were. But after we worked on the math for a while, we discovered that the two entities are actually images of one another—one real, one virtual." He displayed on the auditorium screen a set of formulas, a transformation which proved the mathematical equivalence of the two separate particle-waves.

"Now," March had said with a completely straight face, "and with apologies to Lewis Carroll:

"In the midst of the word we were trying to say,
In the midst of our laughter and glee,
We will softly and silently vanish away—
For the Snark *was* a Boojum, you see."

He and Madison then left the podium.

After the presentation, Spock had heard one normally dignified elder scientist say, laughing, "If they get bored with science they can go straight into stand-up comedy," to which her colleague, who was not quite so amused, replied, "Well, maybe. But the jokes are pretty esoteric, don't you think?"

Spock had made a point of attending their question-and-answer session later that day, and during the week-long seminar became fairly well acquainted with them. He had more in common with Madison, whose intellect was firmly based in rationality, than with the high-strung March, whose brilliance balanced on a fine edge of intensity. But Spock had found their company stimulating; he would be pleased to encounter the two young humans again on Spacelab.

"Spock?" Kirk said.

Spock returned from his reminiscences. "Yes, Admiral?"

"I said: Were they your students?"

"Indeed not, Admiral. They are pioneers in the field

of sub-elementary particle physics. I am honored to have been a student of theirs."

Del March glared at the computer terminal. No way was he going to be able to transfer Boojum Hunt. Every portable byte of memory was already packed full of essential Genesis data, and the team still would have to let some go when they blanked the built-in memory cells.

He had a hard copy of the program, of course, a printout, but it would take a couple of hours for the optical-scan to read it back in, and it always made mistakes. Boojum was a real pain to debug. Well, no help for it.

He was glad they would not lose the program entirely. Boojum was the best piece of software he and Vance had ever written. It was an adventure game; yet it paralleled their real-world work of the last few years. Vance referred to it as "the extended metaphor" but agreed that "Boojum Hunt" was a lot more commercial.

Then Del got an idea. When the storm troopers arrived tomorrow, they would be looking for *something*. It would be a shame to disappoint them.

Vance came over and put his hand on Del's shoulder. "Might's well get it over with, don't you think?"

Del grinned. "No, Vance, listen—don't you think it's about time Mad Rabbit got going again?"

Vance gave him a quizzical look, then began to laugh. He had a great laugh. Del did not have to explain his plan; Vance understood it completely.

Carol returned to the lab. Most of the really sensitive data had already been moved. Only the mechanism of Genesis itself remained. They had another whole day to finish collecting personal gear and to be sure they had erased all clues to their whereabouts.

"I could use a good joke about now," Carol said. She sounded both tired and irritable.

Among other things, she's probably sick of hassling

with Dave about Starfleet, Del thought. He really had it in for them—now he had good reason, but it was hardly his newest theme.

"Vance and I just decided to leave something for the troops," Del said. "The latest Mad Rabbit."

"What in heaven's name is a Mad Rabbit?"

"Do you believe it, Vance? She never heard of us." Del feigned insult. "Carol, we were famous."

"What do you mean,'were'? You're pretty famous now."

"We were famous in Port Orchard, Del," Vance said mildly. "That isn't exactly big time."

"Port Orchard?" Carol said.

"See?"

"What's Mad Rabbit?"

"I'm Mad," Vance said, "and he's Rabbit."

"As in March Hare. We started a minor revival of Lewis Carroll all by ourselves."

Carol flung up her hands in resignation. "Del, I guess you'll let me in on the secret when you get good and ready, right?"

Del started to explain. "We used to have a company when we were kids. It still exists; we just haven't done anything with it since—before grad school, I guess, huh, Vance?"

"Reality is a lot more interesting," Vance said. He pulled a chair around and got Carol to sit down.

Del grinned. "If you call quark chemistry reality."

Vance took heed of Carol's impatience, and as usual brought Del back on track. "We used to write computer game software," he said. "Our company was called Mad Rabbit Productions. It did pretty well. In Port Orchard, we were 'local kids make good' for a while." He started to rub the tension-taut muscles of Carol's neck and shoulders.

"I had no idea," Carol said. She flinched as Vance found a particularly sore spot, and then began to relax.

"The thing is," Del said, "where the game sold best was to Starbases."

"The more isolated the better," Vance added. "They don't have much else to do."

"Not unlike Spacelab," Del said.

But it was true. Spacelab was quite possibly the Federation's least exciting entertainment spot. There wasn't much to do but work. After concentrating on the same subject eighteen hours a day, seven days a week, for close to a year, Del had been getting perilously close to burnout. He had begun having bizarre and wistful dreams about going out to sleazy dives, getting stoned to the brainstem on endorphin-rock and beer, and picking a fight with the first person to look at him sidewise.

He thought he had outgrown that kind of thing a couple of years before.

When he told Vance about one of his nightmares, his friend and partner suggested they revive their old business. It was perfectly possible, on Spacelab, to get drunk or stoned or both, and Vance was not anxious to have to start dragging Del out of brawls again.

"We wrote Boojum just to play it," Del said. "But why not leave it for *Reliant*—"

Carol giggled. "What a great idea. It seems a shame for them to come all this way for nothing."

They all laughed.

The last couple of days had actually been rather exciting. Everyone had managed to convince each other that the Starfleet orders were some ridiculous, awful mistake, and that as soon as they could get through to somebody in the Federation Assembly or in the Federation Science Network, everything would be straightened out. Some overzealous petty-tyrant Starfleet officer would get called on the carpet, maybe even cashiered out of the service, and that would be that. All they needed to do was keep Genesis and the data out of the hands of *Reliant*'s captain until he got bored with looking for it and went away, or until they could recruit civilian scientific support and aid.

Looked at that way, it became a big game of hide-and-seek. It was a change in routine, with a tiny potential for danger, just scary enough to be fun.

"I'll put it in the Monster," Del said.

"Oh, I see," Carol said smiling. "This whole thing is a ploy for you guys to get room to play in the main machine."

"You got it," Vance said.

They all laughed again. They had been working forty-eight hours straight. Del felt punchy with exhaustion and marvelously silly.

Carol patted Vance's hand and stood up. "Thank you," she said. "That feels a lot better."

"You're welcome," he said. "You looked like you needed it."

Zinaida entered the lab.

Over the past year, Del had got used to working with her, but he never had managed to get over a sharp thrill of attraction and desire whenever he saw her. Deltans affected humans that way. The stimulus was general rather than individual. Del understood it intellectually. Getting the message through to his body was another thing.

No Deltan would ever permit her- or himself to become physically involved with a human being. The idea was ethically inconceivable, for no human could tolerate the intensity of the intimacy.

Dreaming never hurt anyone, though, and sometimes Del dreamed about Zinaida Chitirih-Ra-Payjh; in his dreams he could pretend that he was different, that he could provide whatever she asked and survive whatever she offered.

The Deltans, Zinaida and Jedda both, were unfailingly cordial to the humans on the station; they comported themselves with an aloofness and propriety more characteristic of Vulcans than of the uninhibited sensualists Deltans were said to be. They seldom touched each other in public, and never anyone else.

They kept a protective wall of detachment between themselves and their vulnerable co-workers, most of whom were acutely curious to know what it was they did in private, but who knew better than to ask.

Zinaida greeted them and turned on the subspace communicator. Ever since the call from *Reliant,* one or another of the scientists tried to contact the Federation every hour or so. Except for Carol's half-completed transmission to James Kirk, no one had met with any success.

This time it was just the same. Zinaida shrugged, turned off the communicator, and joined her teammates by the computer.

"Genesis is about ready," she said to Carol. "David and Jedda thought you would want to be there."

Her eyebrows were as delicate and expressive as bird wings, and her lashes were long and thick. Her eyes were large, a clear aquamarine blue flecked with bright silver, the most beautiful eyes Del had ever seen.

"Thanks, Zinaida," Carol said. "We'll get it out of here—then I guess all we can do is wait." She left the lab.

Del knew she still hoped *Reliant* might be called off: if it was, they would not have to purge the computer memories. Once that was done, getting everything back on-line would be a major undertaking. The last thing they planned to do before fleeing was to let the liquid hydrogen tanks—the bubble baths—purge themselves into space. The equipment only worked when it was supercooled; at room temperature, it deteriorated rapidly. Rebuilding would take a lot of time.

Jan, the steward, came in a moment after Carol left.

"Yoshi wants to know what anybody wants him to bring in the way of food."

Yoshi, the cook, had put off his leave till the rest of the station personnel returned from holiday. He was convinced the scientists would kill themselves with food poisoning or malnutrition if they were left completely to their own devices.

"He really shouldn't have to worry about it," Del said.

Jan shrugged cheerfully. "Well, you know Yoshi."

"How about sashimi?" Del said.

"Yechh," said Vance.

"I think he had in mind croissants and fruit and coffee."

"Jan, why did he put you to the trouble of asking, if he'd already decided?"

"I don't know. I guess so you have the illusion of being in charge of your own fate. Do you know when we're going? Or how long we'll be?"

"No to both questions. We may be gone for a while. Maybe you ought to tell him we suggested pemmican."

"Hell, no," Jan said. "If I do, he'll figure out a way to make some, and it sounds even worse than sashimi."

After Jan left, Del poured himself a cup of coffee, wandered down to his office, and checked to be sure he had got all his lab notes. The top of his desk was clear for the first time since he came to Spacelab. The office felt bare and deserted, as if he were moving out permanently. The framed piece of calligraphy on the wall was the only thing left: he saw no need to put it away, and it seemed silly to take it. He read it over for the first time in quite a while:

> *Come, listen, my men, while I tell you again*
> *The five unmistakable marks*
> *By which you may know, wheresoever you go,*
> *The warranted genuine Snarks.*
>
> *Let us take them in order. The first is the taste,*
> *Which is meagre and hollow, but crisp:*
> *Like a coat that is rather too tight in the waist,*
> *With a flavor of Will-o-the-Wisp.*
>
> *Its habit of getting up late you'll agree*
> *That it carries too far, when I say*
> *That it frequently breakfasts at five-o'clock tea,*
> *And dines on the following day.*

The third is its slowness in taking a jest.
Should you happen to venture on one,
It will sigh like a thing that is deeply distressed:
And it always looks grave at a pun.

The fourth is its fondness for bathing-machines,
Which it constantly carries about,
And believes that they add to the beauty of
*   scenes—*
A sentiment open to doubt.

The fifth is ambition. It next will be right
To describe each particular batch:
Distinguishing those that have feathers, and bite,
From those that have whiskers, and scratch.

For although common Snarks do no manner of
*   harm,*
Yet I feel it my duty to say
Some are Boojums—

—Lewis Carroll
    "The Hunting of the Snark"

Del sat on the corner of his desk and sipped his coffee. Exhaustion was beginning to catch up with him, dissolving the fine thrill of defiance into doubt.

Vance came in and straddled a chair, folding his arms across its back. Del waited, but his partner did not say anything. He reached for Del's cup. Del handed it to him and Vance drank some of the coffee. He had always had a lot more endurance than Del, but even he was beginning to look tired.

"I can't figure out what to take."

"I don't know, either," Del said. "A toothbrush and a lot of books?"

Vance smiled, but without much conviction. He drank some more of Del's coffee, grimaced, and handed back the cup. "How many times has that stuff boiled?"

"Sorry. I forgot to turn down the heat."

Vance suddenly frowned and looked around the room. "Little brother . . . " he said.

Del started. Vance had not called him that since high school.

"Little brother, this is all bullshit, you know."

"I *don't* know. What are you talking about?"

"If the military decides to take Genesis, they will, and there's not a damned thing we'll be able to do about it."

"There's got to be! You're beginning to sound like Dave."

"For all our Lewis Carroll recitations, for all our doing our amateur comedian number at seminars—hell, even for all the fun we've had—we've been hiding out from the implications of our work. This has been inevitable since the minute we figured out how to break up quarks en masse without a cyclotron."

"What are you saying we ought to do? Just turn everything over to *Reliant* when it gets here?"

"No! Gods, Del, no."

"Sorry," Del said sincerely. He knew Vance better than that. "That was a stupid thing to say. I'm sorry."

"I mean the exact opposite. Only . . . I don't really know what I mean by meaning the exact opposite. Except, we can't let them have it. No matter what."

All of a sudden the lights started flashing on and off, on and off, and a siren howled. Vance jumped to his feet.

"What the hell—!"

"That's the emergency alarm!" Del said.

They sprinted out of Del's office.

Something must have happened when they tried to move Genesis, Del thought.

Vance, with his longer stride, was ten meters ahead of him by the time they reached the main lab. He ran into the room—

Two strangers stepped out of hiding and held phasers on him. He stopped and raised his hands but kept on walking forward, drawing their attention farther into the lab and away from the corridor. Del ducked into a doorway and pressed himself against the shadows, taking the chance his friend had given him.

"What the hell is going on?" he heard Vance say. "Who are you people?"

"We've come for Genesis."

Damn, Del thought. We spent the last two days running around in a fit of paranoia about the military, and not one of us thought to wonder if they were telling the truth about arriving in three days.

He opened the door behind him, slipped into the dark room, and locked the door. He felt his way to the communications console and keyed it on.

"Hi, Del," David said cheerfully. "Can you wait a minute? We're just about to move."

"No!" Del whispered urgently. "Dave, keep your voice down. They're here! They've got Vance and Zinaida."

"*What?*"

"They lied to us! They're here already. Get Genesis out, fast."

He heard a strange noise in the corridor, searched his mind for what the sound could be, and identified it: a tricorder.

"Dave, dammit, they're tracking me! Get Genesis out, and get out yourselves before they find you, too!"

"But—"

"Don't argue! Look, they're not gonna hurt us. What can they do? Maybe dump us in a brig someplace. Somebody's got to be loose to tell the Federation what's going on. To get us out if they try to keep us incommunicado. *Go!*"

"Okay."

Del slammed off the intercom and accessed the main computer. He *had* to wipe the memories before he got caught. The tricorder hummed louder.

The computer came on line.

"Ok," it said.

"Liquid hydrogen tanks, purge protocol," Del said softly.

The door rattled.

"We know you're in there! Come out at once!"

"That's a safeguarded routine," the computer said.

"I know," Del said.

"Ok. Which tanks do you wish to purge?"

Somebody banged on the locked door, but it held. Del answered the computer's questions as quickly and as softly as he could speak. As a safety precaution, the liquid hydrogen tanks would not accept the purge command without several codes and a number of overrides. Del assured the program that he wanted everything purged except for one memory bath.

The banging and thumping grew louder. He was almost done.

"All right!" he yelled. "All right, I'm coming." They didn't hear him, or they didn't believe him, or they didn't care.

"What?" the computer said.

"I wasn't talking to you that time."

"Ok. Codes acceptable. Safeguards overridden. Purge routine ready. Please say your identity password."

"March Hare," Del said.

"Ok. Purge initiated."

A moment later, the computer's memory began to fail, and the system crashed.

A laser-blaster exploded the door inward. The concussion nearly knocked Del to the floor. He grabbed at the console and turned it off. The screen's glow faded as the invaders rushed him.

He raised his hands in surrender.

The tanks were venting into space. In about one minute, nothing at all would be left in any of the station's computers. Except Mad Rabbit Productions' Boojum Hunt.

Four strangers came through the ruined door, three with phasers, one with a blaster.

"Come with us." The one with the blaster gestured toward the exit.

Del raised his hands a little higher. "All right, all right," he said to her. "I told you I was coming."

They herded him into the main lab. About twenty people guarded Vance, Zinaida, Jan, and Yoshi. The strangers, rough and wild, sure did not look like Starfleet personnel.

Vance gave Del a questioning glance. Del nodded very slightly: mission accomplished.

A white-haired, cruel-faced man stood up and approached them. Nearly as tall as Vance, he was arrogant and elegant despite his ragged clothing.

"I've come for Genesis," he said. "Where is it?"

"The scientists shipped out of here a couple hours ago," Vance said. "They didn't tell us where they went or what they took. We're just technicians."

The leader of the group turned to one of his people.

Del recognized Pavel Chekov, and cursed under his breath. Captain Terrell stood a bit farther back in the group. Neither appeared to be a prisoner—in fact, they both carried phasers.

"Is this true, Mr. Chekov?"

"No, Khan." Pale and blank-looking, Chekov spoke without expression.

"Who is he?" Khan gestured toward Vance.

"Dr. Vance Madison."

Khan took a step toward him. Two of his people grabbed Vance's arms. Del saw what was coming and fought to go to Vance's aid. One of the people behind him put a choke-hold on him.

Khan struck Vance a violent backhand blow to the face, flinging him against his captors. Dazed, Vance shook his head. He straightened up. A thin trickle of blood ran down his chin.

"Do not lie to me again, Dr. Madison."

Khan went back to questioning Chekov.

"Who are these others?"

Chekov said he did not know Yoshi or Jan, but he

identified Zinaida and Del. Del tried to figure out what was going on. What were Chekov and Terrell doing with this bunch of pirates?

"You can save yourselves a great deal of unpleasantness by cooperating," Khan said.

No one spoke.

"My lord—"

"Yes, Joachim?"

"There's nothing in the computer but this."

Khan joined Joachim and gazed down at the computer screen. At first he smiled. That scared Del, because it indicated that Khan had either seen Carol's grant application or otherwise knew a good deal about Genesis. The opening Boojum graphics closely resembled a Genesis simulation.

Del looked across at Vance, worried about him.

"You okay?"

The woman behind Del tightened her hold on his throat so that he shut up. But Vance nodded. The dazed look, at least, had disappeared.

Khan suddenly shouted, incoherent with rage. "A game!" he screamed. "What do you mean, a game!"

Yoshi was the nearest to him of the station personnel. Khan swung around and grabbed him.

"A game! *Where is Genesis?*" He picked Yoshi up and shook him violently.

"I don't know!"

"He's telling the truth! Leave him alone!" Vance struggled but could not get free.

Khan set Yoshi down gently.

"This one knows nothing of Genesis?" he asked kindly.

"That's right. Whatever you're after, Jan and Yoshi have nothing to do with it. Leave them alone."

Khan drew a knife from his belt. Before anyone understood what he planned, he grabbed Yoshi by the hair, jerked his head back, and cut his throat. Yoshi did not even cry out. Blood spurted across the room. Warm droplets spattered Del's cheek.

"My God!"

Someone—one of Khan's own people—screamed. Khan reached for Jan. Del wrenched himself out of his captors' hands and lunged. The knife flashed again. Jan's scream stopped suddenly, and arterial blood sprayed out. Del grabbed Khan, who turned smoothly and expertly and sank his blade to its hilt in Del's side.

"Del!" Vance cried.

Del felt the warmth of the blade, but no pain: he thought it had slid along his skin just beneath his ribs.

He grappled with Khan, straining to reach his throat, but was outnumbered. Within a few seconds, they had powered him to the floor. That was the worst show he'd put up since the last time Vance dragged him drunk and stoned and bruised out of a bar and made him promise to quit mixing recreational drugs. He had kept the promise, too.

Weird to remember that now.

He pushed himself to his hands and knees.

Someone kicked him.

Del cried out in shock and surprise at the pain. He fell, then rolled over onto his back. The ceiling lights glared in his eyes. Everyone was staring at him, Khan with a faint smile. Del put his hand to his side, which should have ached, but which hurt with a high, throbbing pain.

His hand came away soaked with blood. That was the first time he realized Khan had stabbed him.

They dragged him to his feet. His knees felt weak, and he was dizzy.

Four people barely succeeded in holding Vance down.

Khan stood just near enough to tempt Del to kick at him, just far enough away to make any attempt futile and stupid. Del pressed his hand hard against the knife wound. It was very deep. Blood flowed steadily against the pressure.

Yoshi was dead, but Jan moved weakly, bleeding pulsebeats. Someone moved to help him.

"Leave him!" Khan snarled." "Let him die; he is worthless to me." He gestured at Del. "Hold his arms."

They already held him tightly, but they forced his hands behind his back. The wound bled more freely.

Khan turned away and strolled to a nearby workbench. "Your laboratory is excellently equipped," he said matter-of-factly, while everyone else in the room, even his people, stared horrified at Jan slowly bleeding to death.

"My God," Vance whispered in fury. "You're insane!" He strained around. "Chekov! Terrell! You can't just stand there and let him die!"

"Be quiet, Dr. Madison," Khan said easily. "My people and I do what we must; as for young Pavel here, and his captain—I own them. I intend to own you." He idly picked up a large tripod.

"My lord Khan, yes!" Joachim said. "Control them completely! There are eels on *Reliant*. I'll return to the ship and get them—"

"That will not be necessary, Joachim," Khan said. "Thank you for your suggestion."

"Sir—"

"Tie them up." He fiddled with the tripod.

Khan's people dragged them to a smaller room down the corridor. There they bound Zinaida and Vance to chairs. Del watched as if from a great distance. He could feel himself slipping down into shock. The whole side of his shirt and his left hip and thigh were soaked with blood. He could not believe what was happening. His reality had suddenly turned far more fantastic than any game he had ever invented.

Del focused on the thought: At least Carol got Genesis away. She *must* have.

Khan's followers flung a rope over the ceiling strut, then dragged Del beneath it and tied his hands. The rope jerked him upright, and he cried out. When his feet barely touched the floor, they tied the other end of the rope to a built-in lab table.

"Khan Singh, my lord," Joachim pleaded, "this effort is unnecessary. It would only take a moment—"

"No. Our dear friend the admiral must know what I plan for him when he is in my grasp."

"But, my lord—"

Khan stopped in front of Del.

"Leave us, Joachim."

He had taken the tripod apart; now he held one of its legs, a steel rod half a meter long and a centimeter through.

"Leave us!" He touched Del's face with his long, fine hand. Del tried to turn away, and Khan chuckled.

His people left.

Jan and Yoshi were dead.

Khan Singh smiled.

Vance struggled furiously against the ropes, cursing. Zinaida sat quietly with her eyes closed.

Del met Khan's gaze. His expression was kind, almost pitying.

"Tell me about Genesis, Dr. March."

Del tried to take a breath. The knife wound radiated pain.

"No. . . ." he said.

Khan hardly moved. The steel rod flicked out and struck Del's side.

It hurt so much Del could not even cry out. He gasped.

"Don't!" Vance yelled. "For gods' sake, stop it!"

Khan Singh did not even bother to ask another question. Slowly, methodically, with the precision of obsession, he beat Del unconscious.

Joachim waited.

Khan opened the door. He gripped Joachim by the shoulder.

"We are close to the prize, Joachim. Dr. March will speak to me when he regains consciousness," he said. "Let it be soon, my friend."

Joachim watched him stride away.

He did not want to to enter the lab. He had heard what was happening. He did not want to see it. But he obeyed.

Dark streaks soaked through March's shirt where the steel rod, striking, had broken his skin. He had lost a great deal of blood, and the stab wound still bled slowly.

Vance Madison raised his head.

"If there's anything human left in you," he whispered, "untie me. Let me help him." His voice was hoarse.

"I have no wish to die as your hostage." Joachim searched for March's pulse and found it only with difficulty. He was deep in shock. Left alone, he would soon die.

Joachim found an injector in *Reliant*'s portable medical kit. He chose the strongest stimulant it offered, pressed the instrument to the side of March's throat, and introduced the drug directly into the carotid artery.

Del March shuddered and opened his eyes.

Joachim had never seen such an expression before, so much pain and fear and bewilderment. He ran water onto a cloth and reached toward him. The young man flinched back.

"I'm sorry," Joachim said. "I'll try not to hurt you." He gently wiped the sweat from March's face. He need not speak to him at all. But he said, again, "I'm sorry."

Joachim had no excuse to delay Khan any longer. Nevertheless, he stopped before Madison and Chitirih-Ra-Payjh. Madison looked at him with the awful intensity of a gentle man driven to hatred.

"Do you want some water?"

"It's blood I want," Madison said. "Your leader's. Or yours."

Joachim ignored the empty threat. He glanced at Chitirih-Ra-Payjh, who had not moved or spoken or opened her eyes.

"Did Khan Singh question her?"

Madison shook his head.

"Tell him what he wants to know," Joachim said urgently. "He'll break one of you, eventually, and the pain will be for nothing."

"You hate this!" Madison said. "You can't stand what he's doing! Help us stop him!"

"I cannot."

"How can you obey somebody like that? He's crazy; he's flat out of his mind!"

Joachim came close to striking Madison, who had no idea what he was saying. For fifteen years, Khan Singh had dedicated himself to the survival of his followers, when he himself had nothing left to live for. Nothing but revenge. Bitterness and hatred had overwhelmed him. Joachim held desperately to the conviction that when his vengeance was behind him, Khan could find himself again, that somehow, someday, Joachim would regain the man to whom he had sworn his loyalty and his life.

"I gave my word," Joachim said.

"When there's no one left," Madison said, "it's you he'll turn on. You must know that."

"I will not oppose him!" Joachim bolted from the room.

Del cringed, expecting Khan to return immediately. But the door slid shut and remained so.

Zinaida opened her eyes and stood up. She flung the ropes aside. Her wrists were raw. She untied Vance.

"Del—" Vance lifted him so the strain on his arms eased. Blood rushed back into Del's hands, stinging hot. The world sparkled. Vance tried not to hurt him, but any touch was like another blow. The stimulant made the pain more intense and prevented his passing out again.

Zinaida loosened the far end of the rope. Vance let him down as gently as he could.

"Oh, God, Vance, what the hell is happening?"

"I don't know, little brother." He gave Del some water.

They heard a noise from the hallway outside. Del froze.

"I can't take any more—" He looked up at Vance, terrified. "If he starts on me again . . . I'm scared, Vance."

"It's all right," Vance said desperately, "it's all right. I won't let him . . . " He stopped. They both knew it was a futile promise.

Zinaida knelt beside them. She touched Del's forehead. Her hands were wondrously cool and soothing. She had never touched him before.

She bent down and gently kissed his lips. Vance grabbed her shoulder and pulled her away.

"What are you doing?"

"Vance, even a Deltan cannot kill with one kiss," she said softly. "But I can give him . . . Vance, I can give him the strength to die. If he chooses."

The strength to die. . . .

Del felt his best friend shudder.

"I—" Vance's voice caught.

"Del, can you hear me?" Zinaida said.

He nodded.

"I'll do whatever you wish."

"Please . . . " he whispered.

She kissed him once more, then placed her fingertips along his temples. His pain increased, but the fear gradually disintegrated.

Zinaida took her hands away. Del felt very weak, very calm. The stimulant had stopped working. Zinaida turned aside, trembling.

They heard Khan outside, his words indistinguishable but his voice unmistakable. Del took a deep breath.

"Damn, Vance," he whispered, "I would have liked to see your dragons."

"Me, too, little brother. Me, too." He eased Del to the floor.

The only times Vance had ever been hurt in a

fight—the only times he ever got in fights—was getting his partner out of trouble. Del tried to reach out for him, to stop him from doing anything stupid, to tell him it was too late.

Just try to stall him, brother, Del thought. For yourself. . . .

But he could not move.

Vance pressed himself against the wall beside the door. Seeing what he planned, Zinaida did the same on the other side.

The door opened.

Vance got both hands around Khan's throat before Joachim shot him with a phaser set on stun. Zinaida clawed his eyes, scoring his cheek, before the phaser beam enveloped her, too, and she fell.

Khan's people lifted Del from the floor. Their hands were like burning coals. Khan gazed straight into his eyes. Del started to understand Joachim's dedication.

"Dr. March. . . ." Khan said.

Del *wanted* to tell him about Genesis. He wanted the hurt to stop, and he wanted Khan Singh to speak a kind word to him—

Del gathered together all the pain and concentrated on it, and gave way to it.

He could see only shadows.

When Dr. March collapsed, Joachim sprang to his side with *Reliant*'s medical kit, numb with shock, and dread of Khan, at his own failure.

Joachim could not forget what Vance Madison had said. As he tried desperately to revive March, he could feel his leader's vengeful gaze.

"He's dead," Joachim said. And then he lied to Khan for the first time in his life. "I'm sorry, my lord."

Khan said nothing to him. He turned his back.

Madison started to revive from the phaser blast. Khan dragged him to his feet.

"I do not have time to be gentle with you, Dr. Madison," Khan said, "as I was with your friend. I have other, more important quarry to hunt down." He drew his knife. "It takes perhaps ten minutes for a human being to bleed to death. If you say one word or make one gesture of compliance in that time, I will save your life."

Haunted by grief, Madison stared through him. Joachim knew that he would never speak.

Khan ordered his people to tie Madison's ankles and suspend him from the ceiling strut. They obeyed.

Khan would make a small, quick cut, just over the jugular vein; the bleeding would be slower than if he slashed the artery, and Madison would remain conscious longer. But he would die all the same.

Joachim could not bear to watch Khan destroy another human being. He fled.

In the main lab, he contacted *Reliant* and beamed on board. He ran to the captain's cabin, which Khan Singh had taken over as his own. A sand tank stood on the desk. Joachim dug frantically through it with the strainer until he caught two eels. He dumped them into a box, raced back to the starship's transporter room, and returned to Spacelab. He ran, gasping for breath, to the small lab Khan had made a prison.

Joachim was too late to save Madison. He stopped, staring horrified at the pool of blood.

Khan stood before Zinaida Chitirih-Ra-Payjh. She met his gaze without flinching; he seemed offended that she did not fear him.

"My lord!" Joachim said when he could speak again. His voice shook. "Khan, they're all too weak to stand against your force—"

"So it seems. . . ." Khan said softly.

"There's no need for you to . . . to . . . " Joachim stopped. He thrust the box into Khan Singh's hands. "She cannot keep Genesis from you now, my lord." He held his breath, for he could not know how Khan would react.

Khan opened the box, looked inside, and smiled. He set it down and put his arms around Joachim.

"You know my needs better than I myself," Khan said. "I'm grateful to you, Joachim; I could not love you more if you were my son."

He *will* be himself again, Joachim thought, close to tears. As soon as this is over. . . .

Khan broke the embrace gently and turned toward Zinaida Chitirih-Ra-Payjh.

Deltans seek out intensity of experience. Zinaida, like most, had concentrated on the limits of pleasure. Some few Deltans preferred pain; Zinaida had always thought them quite mad. But here, now, she knew she had no other choice than to experience whatever came and learn what she could from it. Jedda and Carol and David needed time to get away. She must give it to them. Besides, Carol was convinced rescue was coming. Perhaps, if Zinaida were strong enough, she might even survive until then. She did not want to die. She thought out toward the empathic link between herself and Jedda, and touched it with reassurance. She knew that if she let him know what had happened, he would try to help her rather than escape.

Khan Singh's hand darted into the box his aide had brought him. He drew it out again. He was holding, pinched between thumb and forefinger, a long, slender, snakelike creature. It probed the air blindly with its sharp snout.

"Mr. Chekov would tell you," Khan said, "that the pain is brief."

Zinaida drew back in terror, realizing what they had done to Chekov and Terrell.

This, she could not withstand.

Khan's people pushed her forward and turned her head to the side. The eel slithered across her smooth scalp and over her ear, still probing, searching.

"Jedda—" she whispered. She thought to him all that had happened, so he would know there was no hope, so he would flee, and then she broke the link between herself and her lover forever.

The eel punctured her eardrum. Zinaida screamed in pure horror and despair.

She gave herself to the shadows.

Carol and David and Jedda crept up the emergency stairs toward the main lab. Genesis was safe for the moment, but they were afraid for the others. No matter how reassuring Del had sounded over the intercom, Carol was sure she had, a few minutes later, heard the echo of a cry of pain and fear. David had heard something too. But Jedda kept insisting that everything was all right.

"Dammit!" Carol said again. "*Something's* happening up there, and we can't just run away and leave our friends. Not even to save Genesis!"

"Del said—"

"David, Del lives in a fantasy world half the time!" She wished Del were half as steady as Vance; she would be a lot less worried about them both. If Del tried unnecessary heroics, if the Starfleet people overreacted, he could get himself and everybody else up there in more trouble than they could handle.

Carol reached the main level and opened the door at the top of the stairs just a crack.

Zinaida's terrified cry echoed through the hallway. Carol froze.

Jedda's knees buckled, and he fell.

"Jedda! What is it?"

Carol knelt beside him. Jedda flung his arms across his face, trying to keep her from touching him. He rolled away from her, pushed himself to hands and knees, and slowly, painfully, got to his feet.

"We must flee," he said dully. "Zinaida is dead; Vance and Del are dead. We can't help them."

"But you said—"

"She was trying to protect us! But she's gone! If we don't run, they'll find us and take Genesis and kill us!"

They ran.

Chapter 6

That evening, Captain Spock and Dr. McCoy dined with Admiral Kirk in his quarters. Their argument about Genesis continued on and off, but not at such a high level of reciprocal abuse that Kirk became sufficiently irritated to tell them again to shut up.

The intercom broke into the conversation.

"Admiral," Saavik said, "sensors indicate a vessel approaching us, closing fast."

"What do you make of it, Lieutenant?"

"It's one of ours, Admiral. *Reliant.*"

"Why is *Reliant* here?" Spock said.

Kirk wondered the same thing. Starfleet had said only the *Enterprise* was free and near enough to Spacelab to investigate Carol's call.

He hurried out of his cabin. Spock and McCoy followed.

"Isn't Pavel Chekov on *Reliant?*"

They entered the turbo-lift. It rose.

"I believe that is true, Admiral," Spock said.

The lift doors opened. Kirk stepped out onto the bridge and turned immediately to Uhura.

"Reliant isn't responding, sir," she said.

"Even the emergency channels.. . . ?"

"No, sir," she said, and tried again. *"Enterprise* to *Reliant,* come in, *Reliant."*

"Visual, Lieutenant Saavik."

"It's just within range, Admiral."

Saavik turned the forward magnification up full.

130

Reliant showed as a bare speck on the screen, but it was growing larger quickly.

"Attempt visual communication," Spock said.

"Aye, sir." Uhura brought the low-power visible light comm-laser on-line and aimed it toward *Reliant*'s receptors.

"Maybe their comm systems have failed. . . ." Kirk said doubtfully.

"It would explain a great many things," said Spock.

Joachim, still numbed by what had happened back at the Spacelab, blankly watched the *Enterprise* grow on *Reliant*'s viewscreen.

Behind him, Khan chuckled softly.

With Terrell and Chekov gone, Khan Singh was surrounded only by his own loyal people. Soon his revenge would be complete. Then—would he finally be free? Joachim feared the answer.

"Reduce acceleration to one-half impulse power," Khan said; and then, with a crooning, persuasive, ironic tone, "Let's be friends. . . ."

"One-half impulse," the helm officer said.

The laser receptors registered a signal.

"They're requesting visual communications, Khan," Joachim said.

"Let them eat static."

"And they're still running with shields down."

"Of course they are. Didn't I just say we're friends? Kirk, old friend, do you know the Klingon proverb, 'Revenge is a dish best served cold'?"

Joachim risked a glance at his leader. Khan was leaning forward with his hands clenched together into fists and his hair wild around his head; his eyes were deep with exhaustion and rage.

"It is very cold in space," Khan whispered.

On the viewscreen of the *Enterprise*, *Reliant*'s image grew slowly.

"*Reliant*'s delta-vee just decreased to one-half impulse power, Admiral," Mr. Sulu said.

"Any evidence of damage?"

"None, sir."

"Sir," Saavik said, "if I may quote general order twelve: 'On the approach of any vessel, when communications have not been established—'"

"The admiral is aware of the regulations."

Saavik forced herself not to react. "Yes, sir," she said stiffly.

"This is damned peculiar," Kirk said, almost to himself. "Yellow alert."

"Energize defense fields," Saavik said.

The Klaxon sounded; the lights dimmed. It took only a moment for the backup crew to arrive and staff their battle stations.

"Transmission from *Reliant,* sir. . . . A moment . . . on the short-range band. They say their Chambers coil is shorting out their main communications."

"Spock?"

Spock bent down to scan *Reliant.*

"They still haven't raised their shields," Joachim said. Everything that was happening seemed to exist at a very great distance. Only his memories stayed close to him, terrifyingly immediate, flashing into his vision every time he blinked or even let his attention drift: the expression in March's eyes, the blood flowing down Madison's face, the suicide of Chitirih-Ra-Payjh. And he could not forget what Madison had said to him.

"Be careful, Joachim," Khan said. "Not all at once. The engine room, lock on the engine room. Be prepared to fire."

Joachim obeyed. Two hundred years ago, he had given his word; so he obeyed.

Spock studied the scan results. They were precisely the same as the first set: no evidence of damage.

"Their coil emissions are normal, Admiral." And

then he saw the signal of a new change that was not normal. "Their shields are going up—"

"*Reliant*'s phasers are locking!" Sulu said at the same moment.

"Raise shields!" Kirk said. "Energize phasers, stand by to—"

Reliant fired.

Peter stood ready at his console, wishing, wishing desperately, that he had something he could really do. The ship was on battle alert, with the Klaxon alarm sounding around him and all the engine room crew— the veterans—hurrying to their places or already completely involved in their work. The trainees could only wait at their backup positions and watch. And a lowly cadet could only grit his teeth and try to pretend he was here for a reason.

Till now, Peter had suspected that the whole trip was an elaborate charade, nothing more than a simulation with real equipment. But maybe he had been wrong. Surely, if this were another test, the veterans would stand back and let the trainees handle everything. Peter's heart beat faster. He wondered how Saavik would analyze it, logically. It would be fun to talk to her about it as soon as it was over, whether or not it was for real! He had not even seen her since Commander Scott postponed his math lessons.

Uncle Montgomery had told Captain Spock that Peter could not be spared because there was too much work in the engine room; but to Peter he said that the lessons would resume only when Peter "stopped neglecting his work." Peter recognized the disparity as an attempt to teach him a lesson without damaging his record, which he appreciated—yet still resented, because he did not think that this was a lesson he needed to learn.

He'll quit in another day or so, Peter thought. Maybe even as soon as we're finished with this. *Whatever* it is.

From out of nowhere, a shock wave slammed him to

the deck. A moment later, the noise of the explosion struck. As Peter scrambled up, metal shrieked and a great wind whipped past him. The breach in the hull sucked air from the engine room. An eerie silence clamped down and Peter feared his eardrums had burst. The emergency doors slid abruptly closed, and fresh air poured into the partially depressurized area. Sound returned: he could hear screams, and shrieks of pain, beyond the ringing in his ears.

He grabbed the edges of his console to steady himself. The general alarms moaned at a low pitch.

"Oh, my God!" Grenni cried. His console was alight with warnings. "Pres, we gotta get out of here—"

Peter looked up. Right above them, a heat-transfer pipe hissed thick yellow-green smoke through a crack in the triple-layered unbreakable matrix of the tube. Peter watched with horror. Coolant leak was supposed to be *impossible*.

The radiation signal flashed stroboscopically while the noxious-gas warning hooted. The poisonous coolant gas flooded the trainees' area. Peter's eyes burned. Grenni grabbed his arm and tried to pull him away as the rest of the group fled.

"You're on-line!" Peter cried.

"Shit!" Grenni yelled. He broke and ran.

Peter fumbled for his respirator. He could barely see by the time he got it on. His chest felt crushed.

The primary control panel was damaged, and Lieutenant Kasatsuki lay unconscious on the deck. She was responsible for the auxiliary power main controls that Grenni and Peter were supposed to back up. Now, Grenni's console blinked and beeped for attention. If no one did anything, auxiliary power would fail completely.

The gas closed in around Peter as he overrode the hardware hierarchy and brought his own machine on-line. Despite the respirator, his eyes still teared and burned.

The screams of pain and fear crashed over him like

waves. Commander Scott shouted orders amid the chaos. Peter heard it all, but it was a light-year away; he felt almost as if he had merged with the *Enterprise*—his actions came so smoothly and he knew so easily and so certainly what he had to do.

Back on the bridge, Jim Kirk had his hands full.

"Mr. Sulu—the shields!"

"Trying, sir!"

The intercom broke through the disorder.

"Medical alert, engine room!"

McCoy was already halfway to the turbo-lift. He plunged into it and disappeared.

"I can't get any power, sir," Sulu said.

Kirk slammed his hand down on an intercom button. "Scotty!"

A cacophony spilled from the intercom as every channel on the ship tried to break through.

"Uhura, turn off that damned noise!"

She hit the main cutoff.

Silence.

"Mr. Scott on discrete," she said.

"Scotty, let's have it."

His voice sounded strange: throat mike, Jim thought. He's wearing a respirator! What the hell happened down there?

"We're just hanging on, sir. The main energizers are out."

"Auxiliary power," Kirk said. "Damage report."

The forward viewscreen switched over to a schematic display of the *Enterprise*, with a shockingly large red high-damage area spreading outward from the engine room. Kirk and Spock surveyed the report.

"Their attack indicates detailed knowledge of our vulnerabilities," Spock said.

"But who *are* those guys? *Reliant* is under—who?"

"Clark Terrell," Spock said. "A highly regarded commander, one likely neither to go berserk nor to become the victim of a mutiny."

"Then who's attacking us? And *why?*"

"One thing is certain," Spock said. "We cannot escape on auxiliary power."

"Visual!" Kirk snapped. The screen flashed into a forward view from the bridge. *Reliant,* very close, faced them head-on. "Mr. Sulu, divert everything to the phasers."

"Too late—" Spock said.

In the viewscreen, *Reliant*'s photon torpedoes streaked toward them with an awful inevitablilty.

The blast of energy sizzled through the ship, searing and melting computer chips, blowing out screens, crashing whole systems. A fire broke out on the upper deck. The acrid odor of singed plastic and vaporized metals clouded the air.

"Scotty!" Kirk yelled. "What have we got left?"

"Only the batteries, sir. I can have auxiliary power in a few minutes—"

"We haven't *got* a few minutes. Can you give me phasers?"

"No' but a few shots, sir."

"Not enough," Spock said, "against their shields."

"Who the hell *are* they?" Kirk said again.

"Admiral," Uhura said, "Commander, *Reliant,* is signaling. . . ." She hesitated. "He wishes to discuss . . . terms of our surrender."

Kirk looked at Spock, who met his gaze impassively; he glanced at Saavik, expecting—he did not know what to expect from Saavik. Her self-control was as impenetrable as Spock's.

"On screen," Kirk said.

"Admiral . . ." Uhura said.

"Do it—while we still have time."

The viewscreen changed slowly, pixel by pixel, filling in a new image that gradually took the form of a face.

"Khan!" Jim Kirk exclaimed.

"You remember, Admiral, after all these years. I cannot help but be touched. I feared you might have forgotten me. Of course *I* remember *you*."

"What's the meaning of this?" Kirk said angrily. "Where's *Reliant*'s crew?"

"Have I not made my meaning plain?" Khan said dangerously. "I mean to avenge myself, Admiral. Upon you. I've deprived your ship of its power, and soon I intend to deprive you of your life."

"*Reliant*'s maneuvering, sir," Sulu said very quietly. "Coming around for another shot."

"But I wanted you to know, as you die, who has beaten you: Khan Noonian Singh, the prince you tried to exile."

"Khan, listen to me!" Kirk said. "If it's me you want, I'll beam aboard your ship. All I ask is that you spare my crew. You can do what you want to me!"

Khan lounged back, smiling pleasantly. He stretched his hands toward Kirk, palms up, as if weighing James Kirk, at his disposal, in one, against the *Enterprise* and Jim Kirk's certain but more remote death, in the other.

"That is a most intriguing offer. It is—" his voice became low and dangerous, "—typical of your sterling character. I shall consider it."

He paused for perhaps as much as a second.

"I accept your terms—"

Kirk stood up. Spock took one step toward him but halted when Kirk made an abrupt chopping gesture, back and down, with his hand.

"—with only a single addition. You will also turn over to me all data and material regarding Project Genesis."

Jim Kirk forced himself not to react. "Genesis?" he said. "What's that?"

"Don't play with me, Kirk. My hand is on the phaser control."

"I'll have to put a search on it, Khan—give me some time. The computer damage—"

"I give you sixty seconds, Admiral."

Kirk turned to Spock.

"You cannot give him Genesis, Admiral," the Vulcan said.

Kirk spoke softly and out of range of the highly directional transmitter mike. "At least we know he hasn't got it. Just keep nodding as though I'm giving orders. Lieutenant Saavik, punch up the data charts on *Reliant*'s command console. Hurry."

"Reliant's command—?"

"Hurry up!" Jim whispered angrily.

"The prefix code?" Spock asked.

"It's all we've got."

"Admiral," Khan said, "you try my patience."

"We're finding it, Khan! You know how much damage you inflicted on my ship. You've got to give us time!"

"'Time, James Kirk? You showed me that time is not a luxury, but a torture. You have forty-five seconds."

Mr. Sulu turned toward Kirk. *"Reliant*'s completed its maneuver, sir—we're lined up in in their sights, and they're coming back."

Saavik found the information Kirk sought, but could see no way it could be of use. "I don't understand—"

"You've got to learn *why* things work on a starship, not just how." Kirk turned back to Khan, trying to put real conviction in his dissembling. "It's coming through right now, Khan—"

"The prefix code is one-six-three-zero-nine," Spock said.

He set quickly to work. Saavik watched the prefix code thread its way through the schematics and dissolve *Reliant*'s defenses. She understood suddenly what Kirk intended to do: transfer control of *Reliant* to the *Enterprise* and lower its shields.

"You have thirty seconds," Khan said, lingering over each word.

"His intelligence is extraordinary," Spock said. "If he has changed the code . . ."

"Spock, wait for my signal," Kirk said urgently. "Too soon, and he'll figure it out; he'll raise the shields again. . . ."

Spock nodded, and Kirk turned back to the view-screen.

"Khan, how do I know you'll keep your word?"

"Keep my word, Admiral? I gave you no word to keep. You have no alternative."

"I see your point. . . ." Kirk said. "Mr. Spock, is the data ready?"

"Yes, Admiral."

"Khan, stand by to receive our transmission." He glanced down at Sulu. "Mr. Sulu—?"

"Phasers locked. . . ." Sulu said quietly.

"Your time is up, Admiral," Khan said.

"Here it comes—we're transmitting right now. Mr. Spock?"

Spock stabbed the code through to *Reliant* and followed it instantly with the command to lower shields.

Saavik's monitor changed. "Shields down, Admiral!"

"Fire!" James Kirk shouted as Khan, on the view-screen, cried, "What—? Joachim, raise them—*Where's the override?*"

Mr. Sulu bled off all the power the crippled ship could bear and slammed it through to the phasers.

A thin bright line of light sprang into existence, connecting *Enterprise* and *Reliant* with a lethal fila-ment. *Reliant*'s hull glowed scarlet just at its bridge.

On the viewscreen, Khan cried out in rage and pain as his ship shuddered around him. His trans-mission faded and the *Enterprise*'s viewscreen lost him.

"You did it, Admiral!" Sulu said.

"I didn't do a damned thing—I got caught with my britches down. Damn, damn, I must be going senile." He glanced up at Saavik and shook his head. "Lieuten-ant Saavik, you just keep on quoting regulations. Spock, come with me—we have to find out how bad the damage is."

He strode to the turbo-lift; Spock followed. The doors closed—

Joachim bore Khan's hoarse rage as quietly, and with as much pain, as he would have borne the lash.

"Fire! Fire! Joachim, you fool! Why don't you fire!"

"I cannot, Khan. They damaged the photon controls and the warp drive. We must withdraw."

"No!"

"My lord, we must; we have no choice. We must repair the ship. *Enterprise* cannot escape." He wanted to close his eyes, he wanted to sleep, but he was afraid of his memories and terrified of his dreams. He felt sick unto death of killing and revenge.

—the lift dropped, and the doors opened at the level of the engine room. Kirk took one step forward and stopped, aghast.

"Scotty! My God!"

The engineer stood trembling, spattered with blood, holding Peter Preston in his arms. The boy lay limp, his eyes closed, blood flowing steadily from his nose and mouth.

"I canna reach Dr. McCoy; I canna get through; I must get the boy to sick bay—" Tears tracked the soot on his face. He staggered into the lift. Kirk and Spock caught him. Kirk steadied him while Spock took the child gently from his arms.

"Sick bay!" Kirk yelled.

The turbo-lift accelerated.

Spock stepped onto the bridge. His shirt was bloody —red blood darkening to brown: not his own.

Saavik did not show the relief she felt. In silence, Spock joined her at the science officer's station. As Saavik continued to coordinate the work of the repair crews, Spock slid a roster into the input drive. The information quickly sorted itself across the screen:

ENGINE ROOM CREW: SLIGHTLY INJURED. SERIOUSLY IN-
JURED. CRITICAL.

PETER PRESTON.

Saavik caught her breath. Spock glanced at her—she
felt has gaze but could not meet it.

Saavik's hands began to tremble. She stared at them,
thinking, this is shameful. You shame yourself and your
teacher: must you bring even more humiliation to
Vulcans?

Her vision blurred. She squeezed her eyes closed.

"Lieutenant Saavik," Spock said.

"Yes, Captain," she whispered.

"Take this list to Dr. McCoy."

She swallowed hard and tried to make her eyes focus
on the sheet Spock handed her.

The engine room casualty list—? Dr. McCoy had no
use whatever for it: indeed it had just come from him.

"Captain—?"

"Please do not argue, Lieutenant," Spock said. His
cold tone revealed nothing. "The assignment should
take you no more than fifteen minutes; the bridge can
spare you no longer."

She stood up and took the copy from his hand. Her
fingers clenched on it, crumpling the paper. She looked
into Spock's eyes.

"The bridge can spare you no longer, Lieutenant,"
he said again. "Go *quickly*. I am sorry."

She fled.

McCoy worked desperately over Preston. He had to
keep intensifying the anesthetic field, for the boy
struggled toward consciousness.

The life-sign sensors would not stabilize. No matter
what McCoy did, the boy's physical condition deteriorated. Lacerations, a couple of broken bones, some
internal injuries with considerable loss of blood, a
hairline fracture of the skull: nothing very serious. But
Preston had been directly beneath the coolant-gas leak.
Everything depended on how much he had breathed

and how long he had been within the cloud before the ventilators cleared it.

McCoy cursed. The damned technicians claimed nothing else but this wretched, corrosive, teratogenic, gamma-emitting *poison* had a high enough specific heat to protect the engines against meltdown. Well, they also claimed its protection was fail-safe.

"Dr. Chapel!" he yelled. "Where's the damned analysis?"

Scott watched him from outside the operating room; the engineer slumped against the glass.

Chris Chapel came in, and McCoy knew the results from her expression.

She handed him the analysis of Preston's blood and tissue chemistry. "I'm sorry, Leonard," she said.

He shook his head grimly. Several of the life-sign indicators were already close to zero, and the boy had begun to bleed internally, massively, far worse than before: the sutures were not holding. And would not. The cell structure had already started to deteriorate.

"I knew it already, Chris. I only hoped . . ."

He withdrew from the operating field and changed the anesthetic mode from general to local. Preston began to come to, but he would not feel any pain.

When McCoy looked up again, Jim Kirk stood next to Scott, gripping his shoulder.

McCoy shook his head.

Scott burst into the operating theater. Kirk followed.

"Dr. McCoy, can ye no'—" His voice broke.

"It's coolant poisoning, Scotty," McCoy said. "I'm sorry. It would be possible to keep him alive for another half hour, at most—I *can't* do that to him."

Scott started to protest, then stopped. He knew as well as any doctor, perhaps better, the effects of the poison. He went to Preston's side and touched the boy's forehead gently.

Preston slowly opened his eyes.

"Peter," Scott said, "lad, I dinna mean—" He stopped. Tears spilled down his cheeks.

Kirk leaned over the boy.

"Mr. Preston," he said.

"Is . . . the word given?" Peter stared upward, intent on a scene that existed in his sight alone.

"The word is given," Kirk said. "Warp speed."

"Aye . . ." Peter whispered.

Saavik stopped at the door to sick bay. She was too late.

Mr. Scott came out of the operating room, flanked and half-supported by Admiral Kirk and Dr. McCoy. He was crying. Behind them, Peter's body lay on the operating table.

Dr. Chapel drew a sheet over Peter's face.

Saavik hurled the crumpled list to the floor, turned, and bolted down the corridor. She flung herself into the first room she came to and fumbled to lock the door behind her.

In the darkened, empty conference chamber, she tried to calm her breathing; she fought to control the impossible surge of grief and rage that took her.

It isn't fair! she cried in her mind. It isn't fair! He was only a child!

She clenched her hands around the top of a chair. As if she were still on Hellguard, she flung back her head and screamed.

For an instant, the madness owned her. She wrenched the chair from the deck, twisting and shearing the bolts, and flung it across the room. It crashed against the bulkhead, dented the metal, and rebounded halfway to her.

When Saavik knew anything again, she was crouched in a corner, huddled and trembling. She raised her head.

Darkness raised no barriers to her; she saw the damage she had done.

She was so weak she could control herself once more.

143

Slowly she rose; slowly, without looking back, she left the conference room.

Mr. Scott was unable to speak for some minutes. Finally he looked up at Jim Kirk.

"Why?"

Jim looked sadly at Cadet Preston's body. "Khan wants to kill me for passing sentence on him fifteen years ago . . . and he doesn't care who stands between him and vengeance."

"Scotty," McCoy said, "I'm sorry."

"He stayed at his post," Scott said. "When my other trainees broke, he stayed."

"If he hadn't, we'd be space by now," Kirk said.

"Bridge to Admiral Kirk," Spock said over the intercom.

Kirk hurried to open the channel. "Kirk here."

"The engine room reports auxiliary power restored. We can proceed on impulse engines."

Kirk rubbed his temples, drawing himself away from Mr. Scott's despair, back to the ship and the whole crew's peril. "Best speed to Regulus I, Mr. Spock." He sat on his heels beside Scott. "Scotty, I'm sorry, I've got to know—can you get the main engines back on-line?"

"I . . . I dinna think so, sir. . . ."

"Scotty—"

". . . but ye'll have my best. . . ." He stood up, moving apathetically, speaking by rote. "I know ye tried, Doctor. . . ." He left sick bay like a sleepwalker.

"Damn," McCoy muttered.

"Are you all right?"

McCoy shrugged; weariness lay over him. "I've lost patients before, Jim; God help me, I've even lost kids before. Damn! Jim, Khan lured you here, that's the only way any of this makes sense! He *must* have used your name to threaten Genesis—but how did he find out about it?"

"I don't know—and I'm a lot more worried about keeping him from laying his hands on it. You said it yourself: With a big enough bang, he could rearrange the universe."

"There may still be time. You gave as good as you got."

"I got *beat*. We're only alive because I knew something about these ships that he didn't." Jim sighed. "And because one fourteen-year-old kid . . ." He stopped.

"Shit," he said, and left sick bay.

Chapter 7

The *Enterprise* limped to Regulus I, its crews working nonstop to repair the damage done by Khan. By the time they reached Spacelab, Jim Kirk was able to stop worrying about the immediate fate of his starship; but he became more and more concerned about what he would find at their destination. The space station maintained complete radio silence.

Mr. Sulu slid the *Enterprise* into orbit around Regulus I.

"Orbit stabilized, sir."

"Thanks, Mr. Sulu. Commander Uhura, would you try again?"

"Aye, sir. *Enterprise* to Regulus I Spacelab, come in, Spacelab. Come in, please. . . ." She received the same reply she had received to every one of the many transmissions she had made in the hours since Dr. Marcus's original call: nothing. "*Enterprise* to Spacelab, come in, Spacelab. This is the U.S.S. *Enterprise*. Please respond. . . ." She turned to Kirk. "There's no response at all, sir."

"Sensors, Captain?"

The sensors are inoperative, Admiral," Spock said. "There is no way to tell what is inside the station."

"And no way of knowing if *Reliant* is still nearby, either," Kirk said.

"That is correct, Admiral."

"Blind . . . as a Tiberian bat," Kirk said softly. "What about Regulus I?"

"Class D planetoid, quite unremarkable: no appreciable tectonic activity. It is essentially a very large rock."

"*Reliant* could be hiding behind that rock."

"A distinct possibility, Admiral."

Kirk opened a channel to the engine room. "Scotty, do we have enough power for the transporters?"

"Just barely, sir." The engineer's voice sounded tired and lifeless.

"Thanks, Scotty."

Jim Kirk took his spectacles out of his belt pouch, looked at them, unfolded them, turned them over, then folded them again and put them away.

"I'm going down to Spacelab."

"Jim," Dr. McCoy said, "Khan could be down there!"

"He's *been* there, Bones, and he hasn't found what he wants. Can you spare someone? There may be people hurt."

"I can spare *me*," the doctor said.

"I beg your pardon, Admiral," Saavik said, "but general order fifteen specifically prohibits the entry of a flag officer into a hazardous area without armed escort."

"There is no such regulation," Kirk said. That was easier than arguing with her.

She began to speak, stopped, then frowned, trying to decide how to respond to such a bald-faced representation of a lie as the truth.

On the other hand, Kirk thought, she had a point.

"But if you want to check out a phaser, Lieutenant Saavik, you're welcome to join the party. Mr. Spock, the ship is yours."

"Aye, sir."

"You and Mr. Scott keep me up-to-date on the damage reports." He got up and started for the turbolift.

"Jim—" Spock said.

Jim Kirk glanced at his old friend.

"—be careful."

Jim nodded, with a grin, and left.

Dr. McCoy materialized inside the station's main laboratory with his phaser drawn, the safety off.

Some position for a doctor to be in, he thought—ready to shoot off somebody's head. Jim materialized beside him, at an angle, and Saavik behind them both, so they formed a small protective circle.

"Hello!" Jim yelled. "Anybody here?"

The station replied with the echoes of abandonment and silence.

Saavik went to the main computer and turned it on. She spoke to it, but it did not answer her, a sure sign of a badly crashed system.

"Very little remains in any of the computers, Admiral," she said after working with it for a few moments. "The on-line memories have been wiped almost clean." She loaded the single remaining file, started it running, and watched it for several minutes.

McCoy pulled out his tricorder and scanned the immediate area. He thought he saw a blip—but, no, it faded before he could get a reading on it.

"Sir. . . ." Saavik said.

"Yes, Lieutenant?" Kirk replied.

"This is extremely odd. Only a single program remains. It is very large. It is . . . unique in my experience."

She stood back so Kirk and McCoy could look at the screen display.

"I can make nothing of it."

They frowned at the sizzling, sparking, colorful graphics.

"Another Genesis simulation?" McCoy said doubtfully.

"No. . . ." Kirk said. "My God, Bones, it's a game—if that's all Khan found when he got here . . ." He shook his head. "Phasers on stun. Move out. And *be careful.*"

McCoy moved cautiously down the hall. The lights were very dim, the shadows heavy. Spacelab was enormous: besides the project scientists Spock regarded so highly, the satellite supported and housed several hundred technicians and support personnel. Most of them were on leave now, but there still should be eight or ten people here. So where—?

He caught his breath: a scratching noise, a faint beep from his tricorder. He turned slowly.

A white lab rat, free in the hallway, blinked at him from a dim corner, scrabbled around, and fled, its claws slipping on the tiles.

"I'm with you, friend," McCoy muttered.

Feeling a little easier, he continued. He glanced into the rooms he passed, finding nothing but offices, a small lounge, sophisticated but familiar equipment for a number of fields of study.

If they had to search the entire station, room by room, it would take days. McCoy decided to return to the main lab to see if Jim or Saavik had found anyone.

He opened one last door. Beyond, it was dark.

The hair on the back of his neck prickled. He took a step inside. No strange sound, no strange sight—why did he feel so uneasy?

The smell: sharp, salty, metallic. He smelled blood.

He turned, and a cold hand gently slapped against his face.

"Lights!" he cried, jumping back. His foot slipped, and he fell.

The sensors responded to his voice. Lying on the floor, he looked up.

"My God in heaven . . . !"

Staring at the hanging bodies, McCoy got slowly to his feet. He fumbled for his communicator.

"Jim. . . ."

Five people—a Deltan and four human beings—hung upside down from a ceiling strut. Each one's throat had been slashed. McCoy approached the nearest body, that of a tall black man. His own blood obscured his face. The man next to him had been tortured.

As he waited for Kirk to answer, McCoy gradually got hold of himself. The casual ferocity of the killing gave him a deep, sick sensation.

Jim's voice on the communicator made him start.

"Yeah, Bones?"

"I . . . found them."

"I'll be right down."

"No—! Jim, Dr. Marcus isn't here. *She isn't here.* But the rest . . . they're dead, Jim. Please stay where you are. I'll get a medical team to beam down." He was already trying to think if there were anyone on the ship he could count on besides Chris Chapel to help deal with this horror.

"Kirk out."

McCoy cursed softly.

He took tricorder readings on all the bodies and recorded their position and surroundings. Three of the people had bled to death, one had died of shock, and the Deltan . . . he could detect no cause for the Deltan's death.

What chance is there, McCoy thought, that their murderer will ever come to trial? Not very damned much.

"Oh, my God. . . ." Jim said from the doorway. He stared up, horrified.

"I *told* you not to come down here," McCoy said angrily. "There was no need for you to see what happened." He saw Saavik behind Kirk, her face Vulcan calm. "Or for her to either, dammit!"

Kirk glanced over his shoulder. "Lieutenant, I ordered—"

"I am your escort, Admiral," she said coldly. "Your safety is my responsibility, not the reverse."

"Stay outside, then," McCoy said gently. "Child, it isn't necessary for you to be exposed to this—"

"I am neither a child nor in need of protection."

"Lieutenant Saavik—" Kirk said sharply.

Saavik cut him off. *"Sir.* In order to protect me from sights such as this you would have had to start when I *was* still a child. I will *not* leave you unguarded when a creature who takes such great pleasure in killing—and who would take his most extreme pleasure in your death—is free and in hiding somewhere near. Nor will I stand by idle!"

She paused a moment, looking somewhat abashed by her outburst. She continued in a tone more restrained, but with words no less definite.

"Admiral Kirk, if you in truth prefer an escort who behaves differently, you must order me back to the ship."

Saavik waited, but Kirk said nothing.

She walked carefully across the blood-thick, sticky floor, hesitated a bare moment, and lifted Vance Madison. His body lay limp in her arms, and the rope around his ankles slackened.

"Please cut him down."

Kirk complied.

They lowered the five bodies and found sheets in which to shroud them. Three were Project Genesis scientists, and two were service personnel.

"They even killed the galley chief," Kirk said. His voice sounded stunned.

"The bodies are almost cold," McCoy said. "But rigor hasn't set in yet. Jim, they haven't been dead for very long."

Jim looked around the blood-spattered room.

"Carol. . . ." he said.

The search party returned to the main lab.

Saavik heard a noise. She gazed around the lab, finding nothing. But the small sound came again. She drew out her tricorder and scanned with it.

It wailed plaintively. McCoy and Kirk heard it.

"Lieutenant—?" Kirk asked.

"I don't know, sir."

She followed the signal to a large storage locker. As Kirk and McCoy joined her, she reached out and opened the door.

Two more bodies fell out and sprawled at their feet.

Kirk started violently. "My God!"

McCoy knelt down and inspected them with his medical sensor. One was a dark-haired youthful human, the other an older, bearded man, a captain. Both wore the insignia of the *Reliant*.

"They're alive, Jim."

Behind them, the Spacelab's communications screen glowed on. *"Enterprise* to Admiral Kirk, come in, please," Uhura said.

"Why, it's Chekov," Kirk said.

"Enterprise to Admiral Kirk," Uhura said again. "Please respond."

"This is Clark Terrell, Jim," McCoy said. "I've served with him." In fact he had known him, rather well, for years.

Chekov moaned.

McCoy frowned at the readings on his sensor. Apparently, Saavik thought, they looked as odd to him as they did to her, despite his enormously greater experience.

Kirk turned Chekov over and supported his shoulders. "Pavel, do you hear me? Pavel, wake up."

"Admiral Kirk!" Uhura said. "Please respond."

"Saavik, tell her we're all right, for gods' sake."

"Please acknowledge our signal, Admiral." Uhura's tone became more urgent.

"Some kind of brain disturbance," McCoy said as Saavik hurried across the lab and opened a channel to the *Enterprise*. "It's drug-induced, as far as I can tell."

"Saavik here, Commander Uhura. We're all right. Please stand by. Saavik out."

"Thank you, Lieutenant," Uhura said with relief. *"Enterprise* standing by."

Saavik left the channel open and returned to McCoy and Kirk. *Reliant*'s Captain Terrell was beginning to regain consciousness, and Chekov was almost awake. He opened his eyes and stared blankly at Kirk.

"Pavel, can you hear me?" Kirk said. "What happened?"

"Admiral Kirk. . . ." Chekov whispered. He took a deep breath that turned into a sob. "Oh, God, sir—" His voice failed him, and he cried.

Kirk held him. "It's all right now, Pavel. You're all right. Go on, don't worry; you're with friends now."

Terrell moaned and tried to get up. McCoy hurried to him.

"It's Len McCoy, Captain." McCoy shook him gently by the shoulders. "Clark, do you remember me?"

Terrell's expression was that of a man faced with such horror that he had lost himself in it. "McCoy. . . ." he said slowly. "Len McCoy . . . yes. Oh . . . yes. . . ."

Chekov pulled away from Kirk and struggled to sit up. "Admiral—it was Khan! We found him on Alpha Ceti V. . . ."

"Easy, Pavel. Just tell me what happened."

"Alpha Ceti VI was gone. My fault. . . ."

McCoy and Kirk glanced at each other, both frowning slightly; Saavik, too, wondered how it could be the young commander's fault that a whole world had disappeared. He was clearly still badly confused.

"Khan captured us. He—he can control people, Captain! His creatures—he—" Chekov began trembling. He clamped his hands over his ears. *"My head—!"*

McCoy came to his side and checked him over with the medical sensor. "It's all right; you're safe now."

Chekov's words came all in an incomprehensible rush. "He made us say things—lies—and made us do . . . other things, but we beat him; he thought he controlled us, but he didn't; the captain beat him—he was strong. . . ." He was shaking so hard he could no longer speak. He drew his knees to his chest and put his head down, hiding his face to cry.

Kirk glanced over at Terrell, who maintained the composure of oblivion.

"Captain, where's Dr. Marcus? What happened to Genesis?"

"Khan couldn't find them," Terrell said with dreadful calm. "He found some of the scientists."

"We know that," Kirk said sharply.

"Everything else was gone. He tortured them. They wouldn't talk; so he killed them. The station was too big for him to search it all before he took *Reliant* and went to kill you too."

"He came damned close to doing that," Kirk said.

"He left us here," Chekov said. He raised his head. His face was wet with tears. "We were . . . no longer any use."

"Does he control all of *Reliant*'s crew?" Saavik asked, wondering if humans were that susceptible to mind control.

"He stranded most of them on Alpha Ceti V."

"He's mad, sir. He lives for nothing but revenge," Chekov said. "He blames you for the death of his wife . . . Lieutenant McGiver."

"I know what he blames me for," Kirk said. He sat with his eyes focused on nothing for some moments. "Carol's gone, but all the escape pods are still in their bays. Where's the transporter room in this thing?" He glanced at Saavik.

"Even the Spacelab specifications were erased from the computer, sir," she said. "However, the *Enterprise* should have a copy in its library files."

They contacted the ship, reassuring Commander Uhura and Mr. Spock that they were all right, and had a set of plans for the station transmitted down. Even the decorative printed maps of Spacelab, which ordinarily would have been displayed in its reception area, had been torn down and destroyed.

In the transporter room, Kirk inspected the console settings.

"Mr. Chekov, did he get down here?"

"I don't think so, sir. He said searching such a big place was foolish. He thought he would make the captives talk."

"*Somebody* left the transporter on," Kirk said. "Turned it on, used it, and left it on—and no one still alive remained to turn it off."

Saavik figured out the destination of the settings. "This makes no sense, Admiral. The coordinates are within Regulus I. The planetoid is both lifeless and airless."

"If Carol finished stage two, if it was underground," Kirk said thoughtfully, "—she said it was underground. . . ."

"Stage two?" He must be referring to the mysterious Project Genesis, Saavik thought.

Kirk suddenly pulled out his communicator. "Kirk to *Enterprise.*"

"*Enterprise,* Spock here."

"Damage report, Mr. Spock?"

"Admiral, Lieutenant Saavik would recommend that we go by the book. In that case, hours could stretch into days."

Saavik tried to understand what the captain meant by that. It sounded vaguely insulting, unlikely behavior from Captain Spock.

"I read you, Captain," Kirk said after a pause. "Let's have the bad news."

"The situation is grave. Main power cannot be restored for six days at least. Auxiliary power has failed, but Mr. Scott hopes to restore it in two days. By the book, Admiral."

"Spock," Kirk said, "I've got to try something. If you don't hear from us within—" he paused a moment, "—one hour, restore what power you can and get the *Enterprise* the hell away from here. Alert Starfleet as soon as you're out of jamming range. By the book, Spock."

Uhura broke in. "We can't leave you behind, sir!"

"That's an *order*, Spock. Uhura, if you don't hear from us, there won't *be* anybody behind. Kirk out." He snapped his communicator closed and put it away. "Gentlemen," he said to Terrell and Chekov, "maybe you'd better stay here. You've been through a lot—"

"We'd prefer to share the risk," Terrell said quickly.

"Very well. Let's go."

"Go?" McCoy exclaimed. "Go *where?*"

"Wherever they went," Kirk replied, and nodded at the transporter.

Saavik realized what he planned. She went to the transporter and set it for delayed energize, being careful not to alter the coordinates. Kirk stepped up onto the transporter platform. Terrell and Chekov followed, but McCoy stayed safely on the floor and folded his arms belligerently.

"What if they went nowhere?"

Kirk grinned. "Then it's your big chance to get away from it all, Bones."

Dr. McCoy muttered something and stomped up onto the platform.

"Ready," Saavik said. She pressed the auto-delay and hurried up beside the others.

Spacelab dissolved; around them, darkness appeared.

Jim Kirk held his breath, waiting for his guess to be wrong, waiting for solid rock to resolidify around him forever as soon as the transporter beam ended. Fear tickled the back of his mind. The instant he finished transporting, lights blazed on around him.

"Well," Jim said as the rest of his party solidified, "if anybody's here, now they know we're here, too."

He was in a small cavern: several tunnels led from it. The caverns were definitely dug out, not naturally formed. The chamber was haphazardly piled with stacks of notebooks, technical equipment, peripheral storage cells. It had all obviously been transferred from Spacelab in terrible haste.

"Admiral—" Saavik said. She gestured toward the next chamber. Jim could see within it a massive curve of metal.

He followed Saavik into the second cave. It, too, held piles of equipment, but a great torpedo shape dominated everything.

"Genesis, I presume?" Dr. McCoy said.

Without answering, Kirk moved farther into the cavern complex.

Suddenly someone lunged at him from behind a stack of crates, plowing into him and knocking him to the ground. A knife glittered. Jim felt it press against his throat, just below the corner of his jaw, at the pulse-point where the carotid artery is most vulnerable. When he tried to fight, the knife pressed harder. He could feel the sharpness of its edge. If Saavik or McCoy tried to draw a phaser, he would be bleeding to death before they could finish firing.

"You son of a bitch, you killed them—"

Jim Kirk recognized David Marcus.

"I'm Jim Kirk!" Jim yelled. "David, don't you remember me?"

"We were still there, you stupid bastard; I heard Zinaida scream—"

"David, we *found* them. They were already dead!"

"David—"

Carol's voice.

"Go back, mother!"

"Jim—"

Kirk strained around until he could see her. The knife dimpled his skin, and a drop of blood welled out. He felt its heat.

"Hold still, you slimy—"

"Carol," Jim said, "for gods' sake, you can't believe we had anything to do with—"

"Shut up!" David cried. "Go back, mother, unless you *want* to watch me kill him the way he killed—"

Carol Marcus took a deep breath. "I don't want to watch you kill anyone . . . least of all your father."

David looked up at her, stunned.

Feeling stunned himself, Jim slid from beneath the knife and disarmed the boy. Surely Carol had said that just to give him such a chance—

Out of the corner of his eye, he saw Clark Terrell step forward and take the phaser from the Deltan—Jedda Adzhin-Dall, it must be—who had been covering Saavik and McCoy.

"I'll hold on to this," Terrell said.

Jim stood up and turned to Carol.

"Carol—"

He went toward her, and she met him. She smiled, reached out, and gently stroked a fingertip across the hair at his temple.

"You've gone a little gray—" She stopped.

He put his arms around her. They held each other for a long while, but finally he drew back to look her in the eyes, to search her face with his gaze.

"Carol, is it true?"

She nodded.

"Why didn't you tell me?"

"It isn't true!" David shouted. "My father was—"

"You're making this a lot harder, David," Carol said.

"I'm afraid I must make it harder still, Dr. Marcus," Clark Terrell said.

Jim spun around.

Reliant's captain held his captured phaser trained directly on Jim Kirk and Carol Marcus.

"Clark, in heaven's name—" McCoy said.

"Please, don't move." He glanced toward Chekov, who nodded. He came toward McCoy, who made as if to resist. "Even you, Len," Terrell said. McCoy let his hands fall. Chekov disarmed everyone, then joined Terrell in covering them.

"Pavel—" Jim said.

"I'm sorry, sir."

Terrell opened his communicator.

"Have you heard, your excellency?"

"I have indeed, Captain. You have done very well."

Khan.

"I knew it!" David whispered, low and angry. Jim turned, but not in time to stop him. David launched himself at Terrell. Saavik instantly reacted, catching David and flinging him out of the way with all the force of muscles adapted to higher gravity. They collapsed in a heap as Jedda, too, sprang forward after David.

Terrell fired.

Jedda fell into the beam.

He vanished without a sound.

"Jedda!" Carol cried.

"Oh, God. . . ." David said softly.

"Don't move, any of you!" Terrell's hand clenched hard around the phaser. "I don't *want* to hurt you. . . ."

"Captain Terrell, I am waiting."

Chekov started violently at Khan's softly dangerous voice. He was deathly pale and sweating. He began to tremble. The phaser shook in his hand. Jim Kirk weighed his chances of taking it, but they were no better than David's had been.

"Everything's as you ordered, my lord," Terrell said. "You have the coordinates of Genesis."

"I have one other small duty for you, Captain," Khan said. "Kill James Kirk."

On the ground beside David, Saavik shifted slightly, gathering herself.

No, Jim thought, no, your instincts were right with David. Don't pull the same stupid stunt he did and get yourself killed for nothing, Lieutenant.

"Khan Singh—" Terrell said. He wiped his forehead on his sleeve and pressed his free hand against the side of his face. "I can't—" Wincing, he gasped in pain.

159

"Kill him!"

Terrell flung down his communicator. It clattered across stone. Terrell groaned as if he had been struck himself. He gripped the phaser with both hands, shaking so hard he could not aim.

Pavel Chekov raised his phaser slowly, staring at it with utter absorption. His whole body trembled. He aimed the weapon . . .

. . . at Clark Terrell. He tried to fire.

He failed.

Terrell screamed in agony. He forced his phaser around until he had turned it on himself.

"Clark, my God," McCoy whispered. He reached out toward him.

Terrell raised his head. Jim felt the intensity of his plea to McCoy in his horrified gaze.

The only thing the doctor could do for Clark Terrell now was . . . nothing. McCoy groaned and turned away, his face in his hands.

"Kill him, Terrell!" Khan said again. The damaged communicator distorted his voice, but still it was all too recognizable. "Fire, now!"

Terrell obeyed.

He disappeared.

Chekov shrieked. His phaser fell from his shaking hands, and he clutched at his temples as his knees buckled. He quivered and convulsed on the hard rock floor.

McCoy hurried to his side, pulled an injector from his medical pack, dialed it, and stabbed it into Chekov's arm. Chekov struggled a moment more, then went limp.

"Terrell!" Khan said. "Chekov!"

"Oh, my God, Jim—" McCoy said in horror.

Jim hurried to him.

Blood gushed down the side of Chekov's face. Through unconsciousness, he moaned.

Something—a creature, some *thing*—probed blindly

160

from inside his ear. It crawled out of him: a snake, a worm, smeared with blood down its long, slimy length. Jim fought against nausea. He scooped up a phaser.

"Terrell!" Khan's voice was low and hoarse.

Jim clenched his teeth and shuddered, but he forced himself to wait until the creature flopped on the stone, leaving Chekov free.

He fired, and the creature disintegrated.

"Chekov!"

Jim snatched the communicator from the floor.

"Khan, you miserable bloodsucker—they're free of you! You'll have to do your own dirty work now. Do you hear me? *Do you?*"

After a moment, a terrible sound came from the communicator.

Khan laughed.

"Kirk, James Kirk, my old friend, so you are still— *still!*—alive."

"And still your 'old friend'? Well, listen, 'old friend,' you've murdered a lot of innocent people. Kirk looked at Pavel Chekov lying at his feet, close to death. "I intend to make you pay."

Khan laughed again. "I think not. If I was powerful before, I will be invincible soon."

"He's going to take Genesis!" David rushed toward the next cavern.

Saavik and Kirk both sprinted after him. As they rounded the corner, a transporter beam enveloped the Genesis torpedo. Jim raised his phaser. If he could at least damage it before it dematerialized—

David Marcus was directly in his line of fire.

"David, get down!" Jim yelled.

Saavik caught up to David. He struggled with her.

"Let go—I've got to stop him!"

"Only half of you would get there!"

"Get down!"

Saavik dragged David out of Kirk's way.

Jim fired. The phaser beam passed through the

empty space where the torpedo had been, and sizzled against the stone.

Jim Kirk wanted to scream. He barely restrained himself from smashing his fist against the cave wall in pure frustration. He only had one chance left.

He found Terrell's communicator.

"Khan, you have Genesis, but you don't have me! You'll never get me, Khan! You're too frightened to come down here to kill me!"

"I've done far worse than kill you, Admiral. I've hurt you. I wish to let you savor the hurt for a little time."

"So much for all your oaths and promises, so much for your vow—to your wife!"

"You should not speak of my wife, James Kirk. She never wanted me to take my revenge. So now I will grant her wish. I will not kill you."

"You're a coward, Khan!"

"I will leave you, as you left me. But no one will ever find you. You are buried alive, marooned in the middle of a dead planet. Forever."

"Khan—"

"As for your ship, it is powerless. In a moment, I shall blow it out of the heavens."

"*Khan!*"

"Good-bye, 'Admiral.'"

On board *Reliant*, Khan Singh shut off communications to Regulus I and stretched back in his chair. Not quite what he had foreseen, but a most satisfying climax, nonetheless.

Joachim came onto the bridge.

"Well, Joachim?"

"The Genesis torpedo is safely stowed, my lord. The warp drive is still inoperative, but all other systems will be restored within the hour."

"Excellent."

"Sir?"

"What?"

"May I plot a course away from Regulus I?"

"Not yet. Kirk is finished, but I promised him that I would deal with his ship."

"Khan, my lord—"

Khan frowned at his old friend and aide. Joachim had been with him from the beginning, but he had been acting most strangely since their escape from Alpha Ceti V.

"You are with me, or you are against me. Which do you choose?"

Joachim looked down. "I am with you, my lord." He turned away. "*I* have not changed."

Carol Marcus sat on the floor of the cavern, staring at the empty spot where Genesis had been. She pressed the heels of her hands against her eyes. She could not believe that Jedda, too, was gone. Vance, and Del, and Zinaida, and Yoshi and Jan: all dead. All she had left was David.

She could not help being grateful that it was David who survived. Yet at times she had felt like mother to everyone on the station. She had always been the sort of person to whom people told their troubles.

She grieved for Vance particularly, missing his gentleness, his steadiness. She covered her face.

Despite the pressure of her hands, tears squeezed from beneath her eyelids. She dashed the drops away angrily, forcing back her grief by willpower alone. She could not collapse into the despair she felt: there had to be *some* way to stop what was happening.

She glanced across the cavern toward Jim. She had sworn to herself never to tell him about David, or tell David about him, but telling them the truth had been the only way to keep them both alive. She needed to talk to Jim—to David, too—but since Genesis disappeared they had all three been revolving around each other like satellites, pulled together by her revelation and pushed apart by time and old pain and lack of trust.

"Saavik to *Enterprise*," the young Vulcan—Vulcan?

Carol wondered; maybe not Vulcan—lieutenant said into her communicator for about the twentieth time in as many minutes. "Come in, please."

Carol knew how efficient the other ship was at jamming communications. She doubted Saavik would be able to get through.

She heard a soft moan and glanced across to where Dr. McCoy worked over Chekov, who he had feared might die.

"Jim—" McCoy said.

Jim went to his side.

"Pavel's alive," McCoy said. "It'll be rocky for a while, but I think he's going to be all right."

"Pavel?" Jim said gently.

Chekov tried to get up.

"It's okay, Pavel," McCoy said. "You're going to be fine. Just try to rest now."

"Admiral," Lieutenant Saavik said, "I am sorry, I cannot get through to the *Enterprise*. *Reliant* is still jamming all channels."

"I'm sure you did your best, Lieutenant," Jim said.

"It wouldn't make any difference," McCoy said. "If Spock obeyed orders, the *Enterprise* is long since gone. If Spock couldn't obey, the ship's finished."

"So are we, it looks like," David said.

Carol stood up. "Jim," she said, "I don't understand. Why did this happen? Who's responsible for it? Who is Khan?"

"It's a long story, Carol."

"We've got *plenty* of time," David said angrily.

"You and your daddy," Dr. McCoy said, "can catch each other up on things."

"Maybe he is my biological father," David said. "But he sure as hell is not my 'daddy.' Jedda's dead because of him—"

"Because of you, boy!" McCoy snapped. "Because you tried to rush a phaser set on kill. And it isn't one dead, it's two, in case you've lost count."

"It's more than that, Doctor," Carol said. "In case *you've* lost count. Most of them were our friends. Jim, I think you owe us at least the courtesy of an explanation."

He looked up, and she could see that he felt as hurt and confused as she did. "I'll trade you," he said.

Carol closed her eyes, took a deep breath, and let it out very slowly.

"Yes," she said. "You're right. Jim, Dr. McCoy . . . we may be down here for a while—"

"We may be down here forever," McCoy said sourly.

"—so can we *please* call a truce?" Carol asked.

"I just watched an old friend commit suicide!" McCoy said. "I stood by and I let him do it!" He turned away. "You'll have to forgive—" anger and grief cut through the sarcasm; his voice broke, "—my bad humor. . . ."

"Believe me, Doctor, please, I know how you feel."

"Yes," he said slowly. "Of course. I'm sorry."

When he had composed himself, he returned to the group. They sat in a small circle, and Jim tried to explain.

Carol wished he could give her some reason to hope, but when Jim finished, the implications of Genesis in the hands of Khan Singh left her only despair.

"Is there anything to eat down here?" Jim said suddenly. "I don't know about the rest of you, but I'm starved."

"How can you think of food at a time like this?" McCoy said.

"What I think is that our first order of business is survival."

"There's plenty of food in the Genesis cave," Carol said absently. She shook her head in surprise at herself —she should have led them all there long ago, instead of staying in these cold and ugly chambers. Everything that had happened had affected her far more than she was willing to admit: the clarity of her thought, and her

165

ability to trust. . . . She got up. "There's enough to last a lifetime, if it comes to that."

"We thought *this* was Genesis!" McCoy said.

Carol looked around her at the dark, rough caves piled messily with equipment and records and personal gear. The series of caves had taken the Starfleet corps of engineers ten months in spacesuits to tunnel out: the second stage of Genesis had taken a single day. Carol laughed, but stopped abruptly when she heard her own hysteria.

"This? No, this isn't Genesis. David—will you show Dr. McCoy and Lieutenant Saavik our idea of food?"

"Mother—there's a lunatic out there with the torpedo, and you want me to give a *guided tour?*"

"Yes."

"But we've got to— We can't just do nothing!"

"Yes, we can," Jim said. He casually removed a bit of equipment from his belt pouch and unfolded it. It was not until he fitted its lenses in front of his eyes that Carol recognized a pair of reading glasses. One of her professors in graduate school had worn the same things—apparently, as far as Carol had ever been able to tell, to enhance his reputation as an eccentric. Jim Kirk wearing glasses?

He looked at his chronometer, took the glasses off again, and put them away.

"Is there really some food down here?" he said.

David scowled.

"David, please," Carol said.

He glared at Kirk. "Keep the underlings busy, huh?" He shrugged. "What the hell." He gestured abruptly to Saavik and McCoy. "Come on."

Saavik hesitated. "Admiral—?"

"As your teacher Mr. Spock is fond of saying: No event is devoid of possibilities."

McCoy followed David out of the cavern. Saavik stood gazing at the floor in thought, then abruptly turned and left with them.

Pavel Chekov lay sleeping or unconscious on a pile of blankets.

Jim and Carol were alone.

Carol sat on her heels beside him.

"David's right, isn't he? It's just to keep us busy."

He raised his head. "Why didn't you tell me?"

Carol Marcus had had twenty years to think about how to answer that question, and she had never decided what the answer should be.

"Jim . . . why didn't you ask?"

He frowned. "What?"

"You've known for a long time that I have a son. You know his age, or you could have found out without any trouble. And," she added with an attempt at humor, "I don't believe they take you into the Starfleet Academy unless you can count." The humor fell flat. She did not feel very much like laughing now, anyway. The possibility that Jim Kirk might ask her about David had always existed in her mind; it was one of those possibilities that in the strange and inexplicable way of the human psyche Carol had both dreaded and, on a level she was aware of but never would have admitted to anyone but herself, wished for.

But it had never happened.

"Carol . . . I don't know if you can believe this. I guess there's no reason why you should. But it never even occurred to me that David might be ours. I didn't even know you'd had a child till I got back with the *Enterprise*. And after that I had, I don't know, some trouble putting any kind of life back together. It was like coming to an alien world that was just similar enough to the one I remembered that every time I ran into something that had changed, I was surprised, and disoriented. . . ."

Carol took his hand, cradled his palm, and stroked the backs of his fingers.

"Stop it, Jim. I'm sorry, dammit, I don't know if I'd even have told you the truth if you *had* asked. I swore I'd never tell either of you."

"I don't understand *why*."

"How can you say that? Isn't it obvious? We weren't together, and there was no way we were ever going to be! I never had any illusions about it, and to give you your due you never tried to give me any. You have your world, and I have mine. I wanted David in my world." She let go of Jim's hand. She had always admired his hands: they were square and strong. "If he'd decided to go chasing through the universe on his own, I'd have accepted it. But I couldn't have stood having you come along when he was fourteen and say, 'Well, now that you've got him to the age of reason, it's time for him to come along with his father.' His father—someone he'd never known except as a stranger staying overnight? Jim, that was the only possibility, and that's *too late* to start being a father! Besides, fourteen-year-olds have no business on a starship, anyway."

He stood up, walked away from her, and pressed his hands and forehead against the wall as if he were trying to soak up the coolness and calmness of the very stone.

"You don't need to tell me that," he said. His shoulders were slumped, and she thought he was about to cry. She wanted to hold him; yet she did not want to see him cry.

"David's a lot like you, you know," she said, trying to lighten her own mood as much as Jim's. "There wasn't much I could do about that. He's stubborn, and unpredictable— Of course, he's *smarter*—that goes without saying. . . ." She stopped; this attempt at humor was falling even flatter than the other.

"Dammit," she said, "does it matter? We're never going to get out of here."

Jim did not respond. He knelt down beside Pavel and felt his pulse. He avoided Carol's gaze.

"Tell me what you're feeling," she said gently.

He sounded remote and sad; Carol tried to feel angry at him, but could not.

"There's a man who hasn't seen me for fifteen years

who thinks he's killed me," Jim said. "You show me a son who'd be glad to finish the job. Our son. My life that could have been, but wasn't. Carol, I feel old, and worn out, and confused."

She went to him and stretched out her hand. "Let me show you something. Something that will make you feel young, as young as a new world."

He glanced at Chekov. Carol was not a medical doctor, but she knew enough about human physiology to be able to see that the young commander was sleeping peacefully.

"He'll be all right," she said. "Come on. Come with me."

He took her hand.

She led him toward Genesis.

Unwillingly Jim followed Carol deeper into the caverns. The overhead light-plates ended, and they proceeded into darkness. Carol slid her free hand along the cave wall to guide them. Jim soon realized that it was not as completely dark as it should have been, underground and without artificial illumination. He could see Carol. The reflected light glinted off her hair.

The light grew brighter. With the sensitivity of someone who spent most of his time in artificial light and beneath alien stars, who valued what little he saw of sunlight, Jim knew, without question, that the glow ahead of him was that of a star very like the Sun.

He glanced at Carol. She smiled, but gave no word of explanation.

Without meaning to, Jim began to walk faster. As the light intensified, as its quality grew clearer and purer, he found himself running.

He plunged from the mouth of the cave and stopped. Carol joined him on the edge of a promontory.

Jim Kirk gasped.

His eyes were still dark-adapted: the light dazzled him. The warm breeze ruffled his hair, and he smelled fresh earth, flowers, a forest. A rivulet tumbled down the cliff just next to him, casting a rainbow mist across his face.

A forest stretched into the distance, filling the shell of the lifeless planetoid that had been Regulus I. It was the most beautiful place he had ever seen, a storybook forest from children's tales. The gnarled trees showed immense age and mystery. The grass in the meadow at the foot of the cliff was as smooth and soft as green velvet, sprinkled with wildflowers of delicate blue and violent orange. Where the shadow of the forest began, Jim half expected to glimpse a flash of white, a unicorn fleeing his gaze.

He looked at Carol, who leaned against the cliff next to the tunnel entrance, her arms folded. She smiled.

"You did this in a day?" Jim said.

"The matrix forms in a day. The life forms take a little longer. Not much, though." She grinned. "Now do you believe I can cook?"

He gazed out, fascinated at her world. "How far does it go?"

"All the way around," she said. "The rotation of the planet gives us some radial acceleration to act in place of gravity, to probably forty-five degrees above and below the equator. I expect things get a little strange out at the poles." She pointed past the sun. "A stress field keeps the star in place. It's an extreme variable; twelve hours out of twenty-four, it dims down to give some night. Makes a very pretty moon."

"Is it all . . . this beautiful?"

"I don't know, Jim. I haven't exactly had a chance to explore it, and it's a prototype, after all. Things always happen that you don't expect. Besides, the whole team worked on the design." Her tone grew very sad. "Vance drew the map; his section had a note at the far border, way up north, that said 'here be dragons.' Nobody ever knew if he was kidding or not. Or—

maybe Del did." Carol's voice caught; Jim almost could not hear her. "Vance said, once, that it wasn't worth making something up that was so pretty and safe it was insipid."

She started to cry. Jim took her in his arms and just held her.

Chapter 8

In the storage bay of *Reliant,* Khan Singh completed his inspection of the massive Genesis torpedo. He had tapped its instruction program; though the mechanism itself was complex, both the underlying theoretical basis and the device's operation were absurdly simple.

He patted the sleek flank of the great machine. When he tired of ruling over worlds that existed, he would create new worlds to his own design.

Joachim came into the storage bay and stopped some distance from him.

"Impulse power is restored, my lord," he said.

"Thank you, Joachim. Now we are more than a match for the poor *Enterprise.*"

"Yes, my lord." His tone revealed nothing: no enthusiasm, no glory, not even any fear. Simply nothing.

Khan frowned.

"Joachim, have you slept?"

Joachim flinched, as if Khan had struck him.

"I cannot sleep, my lord."

"What do you mean?"

Joachim suddenly shivered and turned away.

"I *cannot* sleep, my lord."

Khan watched his aide for a moment, shrugged, and strode out of the storage bay. Joachim followed more slowly.

On the bridge, Khan ordered the ship out of orbit. He had calculated carefully to put Regulus I between

Reliant and the relative position the *Enterprise* must keep until it regained power. Foolish of Mr. Spock to transmit the ship's vulnerability to any who could hear.

Regulus I's terminator slid past beneath them, and they probed into the actinic light of Regulus.

"Short-range sensors."

Joachim obeyed. Khan brought the display to the forward viewscreen and frowned. There was Spacelab, broached and empty. *Enterprise* should have been drifting dead nearby in a matching orbit.

It was nowhere to be found.

"Long-range sensors."

And still nothing. Khan stood up, his fists clenched. *"Where are they?"*

In the Genesis cave, Saavik accompanied Dr. McCoy back into the rock caverns. Pavel Chekov had to be moved to where he could be made more comfortable. David Marcus came along to help. They improvised a litter and carried Chekov out of the caverns.

They made the climb down the cliff with some difficulty, but arrived safely in the meadow below. Dr. McCoy made a bed for his patient, who slept so soundly he barely seemed to breathe.

David Marcus lay down in the grass.

"I knew it would work," he said. "If only . . ." He flung his arm across his eyes.

Saavik watched him curiously, if somewhat surreptitiously. David Marcus, it seemed, dealt with grief a good deal better than she did. In addition, despite his original denial, David had assimilated being introduced to his father with considerable grace.

Saavik doubted she would be able to say the same of herself. It would be an unimaginably dreadful event if anyone ever identified the Vulcan family to which one of her parents had belonged. If that ever happened, if they were somehow forced to acknowledge her, the only way either she or they could survive a meeting with honor and mind intact would be for her to kneel before them and beg their forgiveness for her very existence.

And if she ever encountered the Romulan who had caused her to be born . . . Saavik knew well the depths of violence of which she was capable. If she ever met that creature, she would give herself to the madness willingly.

David kept going over and over what had happened on Spacelab. Somehow he should have been able to *do* something; he should have known, despite Del's reassurance, that his friends were in a lot more trouble than they could handle.

He was afraid he was about to go crazy.

He decided to pick some fruit from the cornucopia tree in the center of the meadow. He was not the least bit hungry, but at least that would give him something to do.

When he stood up, he felt Saavik's gaze. He turned around and looked at her; she was staring so hard, or so lost in thought, that she hardly realized he had noticed what she was doing.

"What are *you* looking at?" he said belligerently.

She started and blinked. "The admiral's son," she said with matter-of-fact directness.

"Don't you believe it!"

"I do believe it," she said.

Unfortunately so do I, David thought. If his mother had only been trying to keep Jim Kirk alive, she would hardly have kept up the deception after the fight. It was far too easy to prove parentage beyond any doubt with a simple antigen-scan. If McCoy couldn't do it with the equipment in his medical pouch, then David could probably jury-rig an analyzer himself from the stuff they'd brought down from Spacelab. It was just because the proof was so easy that he did not see any point to doing the test. It would merely assure him of what he would rather not have known.

He shrugged it off. What difference did it make who his biological father was? Neither the man he had thought it was, who had died before he was born, nor the man his mother said it was, had ever had any part in his life. David could see no reason why that should change.

"What are *you* looking at?" Lieutenant Saavik said.

David, in his turn, had been staring without realizing it. He had always been fascinated by Vulcans. In fact, the one time he had met Jim Kirk, when he was a kid, he had been much more interested in talking to Kirk's friend Mr. Spock. David assumed it was the same Mr. Spock whom Saavik had earlier been trying to contact. If David had to be civil to a member of Starfleet, he would a whole lot rather it be a science officer than a starship captain.

Funny he had not noticed before how beautiful Saavik was. Beautiful and exotic. She did not seem as cold as most Vulcans, either.

"I—" He stopped. He felt confused. "I don't know," he said finally.

Saavik turned away.

Damn, David thought, I insulted her or hurt her feelings or something. He tried to reopen the conversation.

"I bet I know who I'm looking at," he said. "Mr. Spock's daughter, right?"

She spun toward him, her fists clenched at her sides. He flinched back. He thought she was going to belt him. But she straightened up and gradually relaxed her hands.

"If I thought you knew what you were saying," Saavik told him, "I would kill you."

"What?" he said. "Hell—trust a member of Starfleet to react like that. Try to give somebody a compliment, and look what you get."

"A compliment!"

"Sure. Hey, look, there aren't that many Vulcans in

Starfleet; I figured you were following in your father's footsteps or something."

"Hardly," she said, her voice and her expression chill. "You could not offer a worse insult to Captain Spock than to imply he is, or even could be, my father."

"Why?" he said.

"I do not care to discuss it."

"Why not? What's so awful about you?"

"One of my parents was Romulan!" She spoke angrily.

"Yeah? Hey, that's really interesting. I thought you were a Vulcan."

"No."

"You look like a Vulcan to me."

"I neither look like a Vulcan nor behave like a Vulcan, as far as other Vulcans are concerned. I do not even have a proper Vulcan name."

"I still don't see why Mr. Spock would be insulted because I thought you were his daughter."

"Do you know anything about Vulcan sexual physiology?"

"Sure. What difference does that make? They still have to reproduce, even if they only try it every seven years." David grinned. "Sounds pretty boring to me."

"Many Romulans find Vulcans sexually attractive. Under normal conditions, a Vulcan would not respond. But the Romulans practice both piracy and abduction, and they have chemical means of forcing prisoners to obey."

She paused. David could tell this was difficult for her, but he was fascinated.

"To lose the control of one's own mind and body—this is the ultimate humiliation," Saavik said. "Most Vulcans prefer death to capture by Romulans and seldom survive if they are driven to act in a way so alien to their natures. The chance that my Vulcan parent even lives is vanishingly small."

"Oh," David said.

"Romulans make a game of their cruelty. A few take the game so far as to father or conceive a child from their coercion, then compel the Vulcan woman to live long enough to bear it, or the Vulcan man to live long enough to witness its birth. That completes the humiliation and confers great social status on the Romulan."

"Hey, look, I'm sorry," David said. "I honestly didn't mean to hurt your feelings or insult Mr. Spock."

"You cannot hurt me, Dr. Marcus," Saavik said. "But as I am not entirely a Vulcan, it would be possible for me to hurt you. I would advise you to take care."

She stood up and strode away.

Saavik paced through the meadow, wondering what had possessed her to tell David Marcus so much about her background. She had never volunteered the information to anyone else before, and she seldom spoke about it even to Mr. Spock, who of course knew everything. The obvious explanation—that she had wanted to be certain Marcus would never speak in a manner completely offensive to Spock—failed to satisfy her. But she could think of no other.

She climbed down the bank to the edge of the stream, picked up a smooth rounded pebble, and turned it over and over in her hand. She marveled at the complexity of the Genesis wave. In a natural environment, a water-worn pebble would take years to form.

She skipped the stone across the surface of the stream. It spun across the current and landed on the other side.

This was without doubt the most beautiful place Saavik had ever seen. It was all the more affecting because its beauty was neither perfect nor safe. She had heard, far in the distance, the howl of a wild animal, and she had seen the sleek shape of a winged hunter skim the surface of the forest. It was too far away for even Saavik to discern whether it was reptile or bird or mammal, or some type of animal unique to this new place.

The only thing wrong with it was that she was here against her will.

She took out her communicator and tried once again to reach the *Enterprise*. But either the signals were still being jammed or no one could answer. And Dr. McCoy was right, too: Mr. Spock should by now have taken the ship and departed for a Starbase. If he could.

She climbed the bank to return to the meadow.

Dr. Marcus, junior, lay on a hillock at the edge of the forest, staring meditatively at the sky and chewing on a blade of grass. The admiral, Dr. McCoy, and Dr. Marcus, senior, sat nearby under a fruit tree, picnicking on fruits and sweet flowers.

Saavik hesitated to invade their privacy, then recognized that if Dr. Marcus and Admiral Kirk wished to be alone, Dr. McCoy and David would have gone elsewhere. She started across the field toward them. She had several ideas she wanted to propose to the admiral. Anything would be better than standing idly by, in paradise or not, while the world they had come from dissolved into hell.

Admiral Kirk seemed so very calm and relaxed. As she neared the group, Saavik unfavorably compared her own reaction to the *Kobayashi Maru* simulation to Kirk's composure in the face of real death or permanent exile.

Saavik wondered again how Lieutenant James Kirk had reacted to the simulation that had shaken her own assurance. Captain Spock had said Kirk's solution was unique, and that she must ask the admiral herself if she wished to know what it was.

"That's what I call a meal," Kirk said.

"This is like the Garden of Eden," Dr. McCoy said with wonder.

"Only here, every apple comes from the tree of

178

knowledge," Dr. Marcus said; then added, "with all the risk that implies."

She leaned forward and put a bright red flower behind Admiral Kirk's ear. He tried to stop her, but not very hard, and finally submitted.

Jim Kirk felt a bit silly with a flower stuck behind his ear. But he left it where it was, picked a handful of bright purple blossoms from a thick patch nearby, and began to braid them together into a coronet. Noticing Saavik's approach—and her pensive expression—he motioned for her to join them.

"What's on your mind, Lieutenant?"

"The *Kobayashi Maru*, sir," she said.

"What's that?" David asked.

Dr. McCoy explained. "It's a training simulation. A no-win scenario that tests the philosophy of a commander facing death."

"Are you asking me if we're playing out the same story now, Lieutenant?" Jim picked another handful of flowers.

"What did you do on the test, Admiral?" Saavik asked. "I would very much like to know."

Dr. McCoy chuckled. "Why, Lieutenant, you're lookin' at the only Starfleet cadet ever to beat that simulation."

"I almost got myself tossed out of the Academy, too," Jim said. He thought about the time, took out his glasses, and looked at his chronometer again. Not quite yet.

"How did you beat it?"

"I reprogrammed the simulation so I could save the ship."

"What?"

Jim felt rather amused to have startled Saavik so thoroughly.

"I changed the conditions of the test." He smiled. He was not a wizard computer programmer himself; fortunately one of his Academy classmates not only was, but could never resist a challenge. It was Jim, though, who had staged the commando raid—or cat burglary, since no one figured out what he had done till quite a while later—on the supposedly secure storage facility where the simulation programs were kept, in order to substitute his version for Starfleet's.

"The instructor couldn't decide whether to die laughing or blow her stack. I think she finally flipped a coin. I received a commendation for original thinking." With a smile, he shrugged. "I don't like to lose."

"Then you evaded the purpose of the simulation: you never faced death."

"Well, I took the test twice before I decided to do something about it, so I suppose you could say I faced death. I just never had to accept it."

"Until now."

"Saavik, we each face death every day we're alive."

Now it *was* time. He picked up his communicator and opened it.

"Kirk to *Enterprise*. Come in, Mr. Spock."

"*Enterprise* to Kirk, Spock here."

Saavik started violently and leaped to her feet.

"It's two hours, Spock. Are you about ready?"

"On schedule, Admiral. I will compute your coordinates and beam you aboard. Spock out."

Everyone was staring at him in shock. Kirk shrugged contritely.

"I told you," he said. "I don't like to lose."

He joined the flower garland into a circle and placed it gently on Carol's hair.

"Energize," Spock said to Transporter Chief Janice Rand. She focused the beam on the party in the middle of Regulus I, increased the power to compensate for several kilometers of solid rock, and energized.

Spock had deduced Kirk's assumptions and intentions. The science officer was curious to know the results of the second stage of Genesis. He suspected that parts of what had been created within the planetoid would be most interesting, considering the odd sense of humor of the team of Madison and March.

He hoped to be able to see it himself and, seeing it, honor the memory of their lives and their work.

The admiral materialized on the transporter platform, and behind him Dr. McCoy and Dr. Marcus, senior, then Lieutenant Saavik and Dr. Marcus, junior, supporting Pavel Chekov between them.

Spock raised one eyebrow. The admiral wore a flower over his ear, while Dr. Carol Marcus wore a floral wreath.

The planetoid must be most interesting, indeed.

Saavik finished saying something interrupted by the beaming process. "—the damage report. The *Enterprise* was immobilized."

"Come, now, Lieutenant," the admiral said kindly. "You're the one who keeps telling me to go by the book."

Kirk suddenly noticed what Spock was looking at, began to blush, and removed the flower. He gallantly offered it to Lieutenant Saavik—who had no idea what to do with it, as no one had ever given her a flower before—and stepped down from the platform.

"Hello, Mr. Spock," Kirk said. "You remember Dr. Marcus—" he presented Carol Marcus, "—and I believe you met David before he also became Dr. Marcus."

David Marcus nodded to Spock and helped Saavik carry Chekov down.

"Certainly," Spock said. "Welcome to the *Enterprise*. I was most impressed by your presentation."

"Thank you, Mr. Spock," Carol Marcus said. "I wish it were turning out better."

Even Spock could see the effects of strain and exhaustion in her face; the deaths on Spacelab must of course have affected her far more than they did him, not only because she was human and he Vulcan, but because she had been far better acquainted with the people who had died. Words of condolence were such a trivial response to a loss of this magnitude that Spock refused to attempt any.

Dr. McCoy went immediately to the intercom and ordered a medical team and stretcher from sick bay.

"By the book—?" Saavik said.

"Regulation forty-six-A: 'During battle . . .'"

"'. . . no uncoded messages on an open channel,'" Saavik said; and then, to Spock, "It seems very near a lie. . . ."

"It was a code, Lieutenant," he said. "Unfortunately the code required some exaggeration of the truth."

She did not answer; he knew she was troubled by the difference between a lie and a figurative interpretation of reality. He knew precisely how she felt. It had taken him a long time to understand that in some cases no objective difference existed, and that any explanation lay completely within circumstances.

"We only needed hours, Saavik, not days," Kirk said. "But now we have minutes instead of hours. We'd better make use of them."

"Yes, sir," she said, unconvinced.

The medical team arrived, and Saavik eased Commander Chekov to the stretcher. She looked at the flower in her hand for a moment, then placed it carefully beside him.

"Jim, I'm taking Chekov to sick bay," McCoy said.

"Take good care of him, Bones."

"What can we do?" Carol Marcus asked.

"Carol, it's going to be chaos on the bridge in a few minutes," Kirk said apologetically. "I've got to get up there."

"Drs. Marcus," McCoy said, "I can put you both to work. Come with me."

Kirk, Spock, and Saavik hurried toward the bridge. Kirk stopped at the first turbo-lift, but Spock kept going.

"The lifts are inoperative below C-deck," Spock said, and opened the door to the emergency stairs. He climbed them three at a time.

"What *is* working around here?"

"Very little, Admiral. Main power is partially restored. . . ."

"Is that *all?*"

"We could do no more in two hours. Mr. Scott's crew is trying to complete repairs."

They reached C-deck. Spock and Saavik entered the lift. Kirk was breathing hard. He paused a moment in the corridor, wiped his face on his sleeve, and got into the cage.

"Damned desk job," he said softly. "Bridge."

The lift accelerated upward.

Jim Kirk stepped out onto the bridge of his ship. It still showed the effects of the earlier skirmish, but he could see immediately that most functions had been restored.

Mr. Sulu, at his old place at the helm, glanced over his shoulder when the lift doors opened.

"Admiral on the bridge!" he said immediately.

"Battle stations," Kirk said.

The Klaxon sounded; the lights dimmed down to deep red.

"Tactical, Mr. Sulu, if you please."

"Aye, sir."

The viewscreen flipped over into a polar view of Regulus I, showing the orbits of Spacelab, *Reliant,* and the *Enterprise.* The two starships were in opposition, one on either side of the planetoid. *Reliant*'s delta-vee coordinates changed as they watched, revealing that Khan's ship had begun a search.

"Our scanners are undependable at best," Spock said. "Spacelab's scanners, however, are fully operational; they are transmitting the position of *Reliant.*"

"Very good, Mr. Spock."

Reliant suddenly accelerated at full impulse power.

"Uh-oh," Kirk said.

It would slingshot itself around Regulus I; unless the *Enterprise* accelerated, too, and continued to chase and flee the other ship, around and around the planetoid, his ship would soon be a target again. And with the engines in the shape they were in, they could not stay hidden for long.

"*Reliant* can both outrun and outgun us," Spock said calmly. "There is, however, the Mutara Nebula. . . ."

Kirk took out his glasses and put them on to study the displays. He opened a channel to the engine room.

"Mr. Scott—the Mutara Nebula. Can you get us inside?"

"Sir, the overload warnings are lit up like a Christmas tree; the main energizer bypasses willna take much strain. Dinna gi' us too many bumps."

"No promises, Mr. Scott. Give me all you've got."

"Admiral," Saavik said, "within the nebula, the gas clouds will interfere with our tacticals. Visuals will not function. In addition, ionization will disrupt our shields."

Kirk glanced over the rim of his spectacles at Saavik, then at Spock. Spock raised one eyebrow.

"Precisely, Lieutenant: the odds will then be even," the Vulcan said.

The crew had taken their battle stations, pushing the bridge into controlled pandemonium. The dimmed lights cast strange shadows; computer screens glowed in eerie colors. Kirk watched the tactical display. *Reliant* was moving so fast it would round the planet's horizon in a few minutes and have the *Enterprise* in line-of-sight. Kirk wanted to be out of phaser and torpedo range yet remain a tempting target.

"Admiral," Saavik asked, "what happens if *Reliant* fails to follow us into the nebula?"

Kirk laughed, though with very little humor. "That's the least of our worries. Khan will follow us."

"Remind me, Lieutenant," Spock said, "to discuss with you the human ego."

"Mr. Scott," Kirk said into the intercom, "are you ready?"

"As ready as I can be, Admiral."

"Mr. Sulu."

"Course plotted, sir: Mutara Nebula."

"Accelerate at full impulse power—" he hesitated until only a few degrees of arc remained before *Reliant*'s orbit would carry it within sight of the *Enterprise,* "—*now!*"

On the viewscreen, the coordinates defining his ship's linear acceleration increased instantaneously by orders of magnitude. The *Enterprise* sped out of orbit.

A moment later, *Reliant* rounded the limb of Regulus, and its course and speed altered radically.

"They've spotted us," Mr. Sulu said.

Dr. McCoy had nearly finished the workup on Pavel Chekov when the battle stations alarm sounded. He experienced an all too familiar tightening in his stomach. For a long time, he had believed his reaction was as simple as fear, but eventually, the better he knew himself, he realized that it was at least as much the loathing he felt for having to patch up—sometimes to lose—young people who should never have been injured in the first place. Usually they were not as young as Peter Preston . . . but they were seldom very much older.

At least—to McCoy's astonishment and relief—Pavel Chekov had a good chance of recovering. The horrible creature had insinuated its long and narrow length into his skull, to be sure; but although it had penetrated the dura mater, the arachnoid membrane, and the pia mater, all the way to the cerebrum itself, it had not, at the time of its departure, actually destroyed any brain tissue. Instead it had nestled itself in the sulci between the brain's convolutions. No doubt it would have done more damage had it remained much longer, but as it was Chekov should convalesce as if from a severe concussion. McCoy found no evidence of infection. Pavel Chekov was a very fortunate man.

The ship shuddered around him.

"What was that?" David Marcus had been pacing back and forth through sick bay, nervous as a cat, haunted. Just now there was very little to do. If they were lucky, things would continue that way.

"Impulse engines," McCoy said.

"What does that mean?"

"Well, son, I expect it means the chase is on."

"I'm going up there."

"To the bridge? No, you're not. You'd just be in the way. Best stay here, David."

"Dammit—there must be something I can do."

"There isn't," McCoy said. "Nor anything I can do. All we can do is wait for them to start shooting at each other, and wish we could keep them from doing it. That's the trouble with this job."

Khan Singh chuckled at the pitiful attempt of the *Enterprise* to evade him. *Reliant,* accelerating under full impulse power, streaked out of orbit after James Kirk's crippled ship.

"So," he said to Joachim. "They are not so wounded as they wished us to believe. The hunt will be better than I thought, my friend."

Joachim displayed a long-range scan of their course, showing the *Enterprise* and the great opaque cloud of the nebula ahead.

"My lord, we will lose our advantage if we follow them into the dust. I beg you—"

Khan cut him off. Joachim was beginning to sound like a traitor. Khan decided to give him one last chance.

"Rake the *Enterprise,*" he ordered.

The phaser rippled outward, a long finger of dense light. It streaked along the side of the *Enterprise*'s starboard engine nacelle. The starship heeled over and began to tumble, spiraling on its headlong course.

The *Enterprise* lurched; its artificial gravity flexed, trembled, and finally steadied. McCoy closed his eyes a moment, till he regained his balance.

Action commenced, he thought bitterly.

Chekov gave an inarticulate cry and sat up abruptly, his eyes wild.

"Take it easy," McCoy said.

"I must help Captain—"

"*No*. Listen to me, Pavel. You've been through a hell of a lot. You haven't any strength, and you haven't any equilibrium."

"But—"

"You can lie down willingly, or you can lie down sedated. Which will it be?"

Pavel tried again to get up. He nearly passed out. McCoy caught him and eased him back on the bed. The young Russian turned deathly pale.

"*Now* will you stay put?"

Chekov nodded slightly without opening his eyes.

The ship shuddered again. Coming out of the instrument room where she had been helping Chris Chapel, Carol Marcus staggered, then recovered her balance. The flower garland slipped from her hair. She caught it, stared at it as if she had never seen it before, and carefully laid it aside.

"Dr. McCoy, I can't just sit here. I keep thinking about— Please, give me something to do."

"Like I was tellin' David," McCoy said grimly, "there isn't much *to* do. . . ." He realized how desperate she was to stay occupied. "But you can help me get the surgery ready. I'm expecting customers."

Marcus paled, but she did not back off.

If what she and the kid have been through in the last couple of days didn't break them, I guess nothing will, McCoy thought.

Marcus glanced around sick bay.

"Where *is* David?" she said.

"I don't know—he was here a minute ago."

"Ion concentration increasing," Mr. Spock said. "Approximately two minutes to sensor overload and shield shutdown."

The ship plowed on. Encountering great quantities of ionized dust and gases, the shields began to re-radiate energy in the visual spectrum. The viewscreen picked it up, sparkling and shimmering. The crisp rustle of static rose over the low hum of conversation and information on the bridge. A tang of ozone filled the air.

Reliant fired again. The *Enterprise* shuddered. If the shields were not quite steady, at least they held.

"*Reliant* is closing fast," Saavik said.

Directly ahead, the nebula's core raged.

"They just don't want us going in there," Kirk said, nodding toward the viewscreen.

"One minute," Spock said.

The turbo-lift doors slipped open, and David Marcus came onto the bridge.

"Admiral, *Reliant* is decelerating."

"Uhura, patch me in."

"Aye, sir."

Khan felt the power of the impulse engines slacken, then whisper into reverse thrust. The gap between *Reliant* and the *Enterprise* immediately widened.

"Joachim, why are we decelerating?"

"My lord, we daren't follow them into the nebula. Our shields will fail—"

"Khan, this is James Kirk."

Khan Singh leaped to his feet with a scream of surprise and anger. James Kirk—still alive!

"We tried it your way, Khan. Are you game for a rematch?"

Khan struggled to gain control over his rage.

James Kirk began to laugh. "Superior intellect!" he said with contempt. "You're a fool, Khan. A brutal, murderous, ridiculous fool."

"Full impulse power!" Khan's voice was a growl.

Joachim stood up and faced him. "My lord, no! You have everything! You have Genesis!" He looked Khan in the eye, and this time he did not flinch. Khan strode toward the helm, but Joachim blocked his way.

"My lord—" he said, pleading.

"Full power!" Khan cried.

He struck his friend with the violent strength of fury. The blow lifted Joachim completely off the deck and flung him over the control console. He fell hard against the forward bulkhead, lay still for a moment, then dragged himself to his feet.

"Full power, damn you!" Khan grabbed the controls and slammed full power to the engines.

Spock watched the tactical display. *Reliant* stopped decelerating and plunged forward at full impulse power.

"Khan Singh does have at least one admirable quality," the Vulcan said.

"Oh?" said Kirk. "And what's that?"

"He is extremely consistent." Spock glanced at the ionization readings. The ship had technically been within the nebula for some time. Now it approached a thick band of dust where pressure waves from the original exploding star met and interfered. The energy flux and mass concentration must disrupt the *Enterprise*'s operation.

"They're following us," said Mr. Sulu.

"Sensor overload . . . mark." Almost immediately, the image on the viewscreen broke up and shattered.

Sulu piloted the ship blind through the cloud of gas and dust and energy.

Joachim returned to his place at the helm, bewildered into obedience. In all the years that he had served his lord, all the times of witnessing the violence to which Khan was prone, Joachim had never himself been subject to that wrath. Khan had never assaulted him. Until now.

Joachim had been in fights aplenty; he had even, in his younger days, lost a few. None had ever affected him like the single blow from Khan Singh. His hands shook on the controls, partly from humiliation and partly from rage. He had sworn to follow Khan even to death. There was no room for compromise: he had put no conditions on his vow. No conditions for madness, no conditions for betrayal.

Freedom was in Khan's grasp; yet he was throwing it away. Joachim indeed felt betrayed.

The *Enterprise* vanished into a thick projection of dust, a tendril of exploded matter from the pulsar at the nova's center.

"Follow it!" Khan said.

Joachim held his tongue and obeyed.

The viewscreen's image dissolved into random colors, punctuated by the periodic flash of the pulsar's electromagnetic field.

"Tactical!" Khan cried.

"Inoperative," Joachim said without expression.

"Raise the shields!"

"Inoperative." Joachim saw that the ship's hull could not long withstand the stress of the high concentration of dust, not at the speed it was going. "Reducing speed," he said coldly.

He could feel Khan's gaze burning into him, but this time Khan made no protest.

The *Enterprise* broke through the worst of the dust; visuals and tacticals returned, but the shields were out completely. Sulu changed course, creeping through the nebula's diffuse mass just outside the irregular boundary which would both hide the *Enterprise* and blind it.

The *Enterprise* hovered outside the cloud and waited.

"Here it comes," Saavik said.

Reliant plowed slowly through the dust. It would be blind for another few moments.

"Phaser lock just blew, Admiral," Mr. Sulu said.

"Do your best, Mr. Sulu. Fire when ready."

Sulu believed he could hit the opposing ship, even at this range. Precisely, carefully, he aimed. A moment's pause:

Fire—

The magnetic bearings of a stabilizing gyro exploded, and the *Enterprise* lurched. The phasers beam went wide.

Sulu muttered a curse and plunged the *Enterprise* back into the nebula as *Reliant* spotted them and fired. The photon torpedo just missed, but it expended its energy in the cloud, and a mass of charged particles and radiation slammed into them. He struggled to steady the ship.

"Hold your course," Kirk said. "Look sharp. . . ."

"At *what?*" Lieutenant Saavik murmured. She drew more power to the sensors, tightened the angle, and ran the input through enhancement.

For an instant, the viewscreen cleared. Sulu started involuntarily—*Reliant* loomed on the screen: collision course!

"Evasive starboard!" Kirk yelled.

Too late.

Reliant's phaser blast hit the unshielded *Enterprise* dead-on. The power-surge baffles on the primary helm console failed completely. It carried a jolt of electricity straight through the controls. Half the instruments blew out. Sulu felt the voltage arc across his hands. It flung him back, arching his spine and shaking him like a great ferocious animal, and slammed him to the deck.

Every muscle in Sulu's body cramped into knots. He lurched over onto his face and tried to rise. He could not breathe. The pain from his seared hands shot through him, cold and hot and overwhelming.

He lost consciousness.

When Mr. Sulu fell, Saavik leaped to the helm, seeking out which operations still functioned and which had crashed.

"Phaser bank one!" Kirk said. "Fire!"

Saavik's hands were an extension of the controls, her body was part of the ship itself.

She fired.

* * *

The *Enterprise*'s phaser beam sizzled across *Reliant*'s main hull, full force. The blast reverberated across the bridge. Power failed for a moment, and with it artificial gravity and all illumination. Khan gripped the armrests of the captain's chair, holding himself steady, but through the darkness and the shrieks of tortured metal he heard his people cry out and fall.

Joachim pitched forward over the helm controls.

"Joachim!"

The gravity flowed back, returning slowly to normal, and the lights glowed to a bare dimness.

As *Reliant* plunged ahead, unpiloted and blind, Khan sprang to his old friend's side. He lifted him as gently as he could. Joachim cried out in pain. Khan lowered him to the deck, supporting his shoulders. The jagged ends of broken bones ground together, and Joachim's face was bloody and lacerated. He reached out, his fingers spread and searching.

He could not see.

Khan permitted the touch. He laid his hand over Joachim's.

"My lord. . . ." Joachim whispered. "You proved . . . yourself . . . superior. . . ."

Khan could feel the life ebbing from his friend. For a moment, he experienced despair. His sight blurred: he tried to force away the tears, but they spilled unchecked down his face. This was what his hatred had bought—

James Kirk would repay the price.

"I shall avenge you," Khan said to Joachim, his voice a growl.

"I wished . . . no . . . revenge. . . ."

Khan laid his friend down carefully. He stood up, his fists clenched at his side.

"I shall avenge you."

After taking the *Enterprise*'s phaser burst, *Reliant* shot away dead straight, without a maneuver. David Marcus thought the *Enterprise* had won. Yet there was no elation from the bridge crew, only concentration on the scattery viewscreen, murmured interchanges of essential information, and tension over all, like a sound pitched just above the range of hearing.

Kirk spoke into the intercom. "Get a medic up here! Stat!"

David pulled himself out of his observer's detachment and hurried to the side of the injured helm officer.

Sulu was not breathing. His hands were badly burned, and his skin was clammy. David felt his throat for a pulse and got absolutely nothing.

David Marcus was not a medical doctor. He knew some first aid, which he had never had to use. He took a deep breath. The air was heavy with the smell of burned plastic and vaporized metal.

He tilted Sulu's head back, opened his mouth, breathed four breaths into him, pressed the heels of his hands over the helm officer's sternum, and compressed his chest rapidly fifteen times in a row. A breath, fifteen compressions. Sulu did not react, but David kept going. A breath, fifteen compressions.

"What's the damage, Scotty?" he heard Kirk say.

For David, everything was peripheral except the life in his hands. The first rule of manual cardiopulmonary resuscitation was and always had been: Don't stop. No matter what, don't stop.

A breath, fifteen compressions.

"Admiral," the engineer said, "I canna put the mains back on-line! The energizer's burst; if I try to gi' it to ye, 'twill go critical!"

"Scotty, we've got to have main power! Get in there and fix it!"

A breath, fifteen compressions. David's shoulders and arms were beginning to ache.

"It isna possible, sir!" Mr. Scott cried. "The radiation level is far too high; i' ha' already burned out the electronics o' the repair robot, and if ye went in in a suit 'twould freeze for the same reason! A person unprotected wouldna last a minute!"

A breath, fifteen compressions. The ache in David's shoulders crept slowly into pain. Sweat rolled down his forehead and stung in his eyes. He could not stop to wipe it away.

"How long, Scotty?"

"I canna say, sir. Decontamination is begun, but 'twill be a while—"

A breath, fifteen compressions. David was breathing heavily himself now. He had not realized what lousy condition he was in. He had worked long hours on Spacelab, but it was essentially a sedentary job; the only exercise he had ever got was playing zero-gee handball with Zinaida, whom he had sometimes accused of using him as a moving wall to bounce the ball off of.

Come on, Sulu, he thought, give me a little help, man, please.

A breath, fifteen compressions.

The turbo-lift doors slid open, and a medical team hurried onto the bridge.

"Hurry—up—you—guys—" David said.

A medic vaulted down the stairs and knelt beside him.

"Any reaction?"

David shook his head. His sweat-damp hair plastered itself against his forehead.

"Keep going," the medic said. She drew a pressure-injector out of her bag, dialed it, and fitted a long, heavy needle to it. "I'm going to try epinephrine straight to the heart. When I tell you, get out of my way but keep breathing for him. Okay?"

David could hardly see because of the sweat sparkling in his eyes. He nodded. The medic ripped Sulu's shirt open, baring his chest. The fabric parted beneath David's hands.

"Okay. Now!"

He moved quickly, sliding aside but continuing to breathe for the helm officer. What was the count for artificial respiration? Fifteen per minute? He held Sulu's head just beneath his jaw but still could feel no pulse.

The medic plunged the needle down.

The reaction was almost instantaneous. Sulu shuddered, and his clammy skin flushed. David felt a pulse, thready and fast. Sulu gasped. David did not know what to do, whether to stop or keep going.

The medic took his shoulder. "It's okay," she said. "You can stop now."

David stopped. He could barely raise his head. He was dripping with sweat and panting. But Sulu was breathing on his own.

"Good work," the medic said.

"How is he?" Kirk said without taking his gaze off the viewscreen.

"Can't tell yet," the medic said. "He's alive, thanks to his friend here."

She flung out a stretcher. It rippled, straightened, solidified. David staggered to his feet and tried to help her get Sulu onto it. He was not a great deal of use in lifting, because his arms were so tired they had gone numb. But once Sulu was on the stretcher, David at least could guide it. While the medic started working on Sulu's burns, David pushed the stretcher to the turbo-lift and down to sick bay.

Pavel Chekov felt and heard the battle begin; he watched the flow of casualties start and increase. He considered himself responsible for everything that had happened. He tried to sit up, but Dr. McCoy had strapped him down—it was a safety precaution, not restraint, and as the ship rocked and shuddered around him he freed his arms and fumbled for the fastenings. Sick bay spun around him; he had to close his eyes again to get his balance.

For a moment, he lay back. What possible use could he be on the bridge, half-crippled and sick?

Then they brought Mr. Sulu in. Dr. Chapel read his life signs grimly, looked at his hands, and cursed under her breath.

Chekov ripped off the restraining straps and forced himself to stand. In the confusion, no one noticed him get up; or if they did, they did not try to make him lie down again.

His hearing was still one-sided. At the entrance to sick bay, he lost his balance and kept from falling only by grabbing the doorjamb.

Someone took him by the shoulder.

"You'd better lie down again," David Marcus said. Chekov remembered him vaguely and dimly from the painful haze of Regulus I.

"I can't," Chekov said. "I must get to bridge—Mr. Sulu—"

"Hey, look—"

"Pozhalusta," Chekov said, "help me. *Bozhe moi!* The ship has nothing but children on its crew!"

David hesitated. Chekov wondered if he would have to try to fight him to get out of sick bay.

David slung Chekov's arm across his shoulder and helped him toward the lift.

Chekov would never have made it to the bridge without Marcus's help. Even half-supported, he felt like he was struggling through a whirlpool.

As the lift doors opened, Chekov drew away from David Marcus: Admiral Kirk would send him back if he could not even make it to the bridge on his own feet. David seemed to understand, and let him go without argument.

Chekov walked carefully across the upper level, took a deep breath, and managed to navigate the stairs without falling. At Kirk's elbow, he stopped.

"Sir, could you use another hand?"

Kirk glanced at him, startled. Then he smiled.

"Take your place at the weapons console, Mr. Chekov."

"Thank you, sir."

At the science officer's station, Mr. Spock tried to make something of the distorted readings his sensors were receiving.

"Spock, can you find him?"

"The energy readings are sporadic and indeterminate, but they could indicate extreme radial acceleration under full impulse power. Port side, aft."

"He won't stop now," Kirk said. "He's followed me this far; he'll be back. But where the hell *from?*"

Spock considered.

"Admiral," he said. "Khan's intelligence cannot make up for his lack of experience. All the maneuvering *Reliant* has done, bold though it may be, has occurred in a single plane. He takes advantage neither of the full abilities of his ship nor of the possibilities inherent in three degrees of freedom."

Kirk glanced back at him and grinned. "A masterful analysis, Mr. Spock. Lieutenant Saavik, all stop."

Saavik decelerated the ship to zero relative motion.

"All stop, sir."

"Full thrust ninety degrees from our previous course: straight down."

"Aye, sir."

"Mr. Chekov, stand by photon torpedoes."

"Aye, sir."

The *Enterprise* plunged downward into the shadows of the nebula.

Khan sought any sign of Kirk in the mangled image on his viewscreen. All around him lay the wreckage of the bridge and the bodies of his people. A few moaned, still alive, but he no longer cared. This was a battle to the death. He would be glad to die if he took James Kirk with him.

He scanned the space surrounding *Reliant,* but found nothing. Nothing at all—only the impenetrable energy fields of the nebula.

"Where is Kirk?" he cried. "Where in the land of Hades is he?"

Nothing, no one, replied.

The *Enterprise* hovered within the Mutara Nebula's great dustcloud. The ship was blind and deaf. Jim Kirk forced himself to sit quiet and relaxed as if nothing worried him. It was the biggest act of his life. The ship was badly hurt; every score of *Reliant*'s weapons had touched him as painfully as any physical blow. And in truth, he had no idea what Khan would try next. He could only estimate, and guess, and hope.

At the helm, Saavik glanced at him with a questioning expression.

"Hold steady, Lieutenant," he said.

She nodded once and turned back to her position. Chekov never moved. He hunched over Sulu's weapons console. He had looked terrible when he came in, pale and sick and dizzy. But the truth was Kirk needed him; the ship needed him. With Sulu gone— Kirk glanced around the bridge and saw that David had returned. He gestured to him. The young man came down the stairs and stopped beside the captain's seat.

"How's Sulu?"

"They don't know yet," David said. "His hands are a mess—he'll be in therapy for a while. If he lives. They wouldn't say. He might have brain damage."

"You got to him fast," Jim said. "He'd be dead if you hadn't. You gave him the one chance he had. Whatever happens—David, I'm proud of you."

To Jim's surprise and shock, David reacted with a curse.

"What the hell right have you got to be proud of me?" he said angrily.

He stormed back to the upper level of the bridge and stood scowling with his arms folded across his chest. He ignored Jim Kirk's gaze.

Jim turned back to the viewscreen, angry and hurt.

"Stand by photon torpedoes," he snapped at Chekov.

"Photon torpedoes ready, sir."

The interchange with David had broken Jim's concentration. He felt irritated and foolish to have tried to make peace and friends with the boy and to have been so throughly rebuffed. It served him right for thinking about personal matters when the ship was in danger. He forced himself back to the problem at hand.

"Lieutenant Saavik."

"Aye, sir."

He had been tempted to say, "Dive! dive! dive!" earlier, but refrained; now he kept himself from ordering the young Vulcan officer to let the ship surface. This was not, after all, a submarine, and they were not hunting an enemy U-boat.

Too many old novels, Jim, he thought.

If he failed, his crew would have not a comforting sea to receive them, but unforgiving vacuum filled with nothing but radiation.

"Accelerate. Full impulse power at course zero and plus ninety. Just until the sensors clear." That would get them out of the worst of the dust. "Then all stop."

"Aye, sir," she said, and executed the command.

The artificial gravity was holding, but at a level tentative enough that Kirk could feel the acceleration: straight up. The viewscreen was still dead, but as they rose out of the gas cloud it slowly cleared.

The roiling mass of dust and gases draped away from Jim Kirk's ship like the sea around the flanks of a huge ocean mammal. They rose: and *Reliant* lay full ahead.

Bull's-eye! Jim Kirk thought.

"Mr. Chekov—!"

"Torpedoes ready, sir!"

"Fire!"

Chekov fired.

The torpedoes streaked away.

In the pure silence of hard vacuum, the torpedoes

touched the enemy ship and exploded. *Reliant*'s starboard engine nacelle collapsed, spun, tumbled, and gracefully, quietly, exploded.

Reliant responded not at all. The ship drifted steady on its course.

"Cease fire," Kirk said. "Look sharp."

The bridge crew reacted with silence, watching, waiting. Too soon to be certain. . . .

"Match course, Lieutenant," Kirk said to Saavik.

She obeyed: the *Enterprise* followed *Reliant*, maneuvering slightly till their relative speeds were zero, and *Reliant* appeared dead in space.

"Our power levels are extremely low, sir," Lieutenant Saavik said.

Kirk switched the intercom to the engine room. "Mr. Scott, how long before you can get the mains back on-line?"

"At least ten minutes, sir, I canna send anyone in till after decontamination."

Kirk glowered and snapped the channel off. "Commander Uhura, send to Commander, *Reliant:* Prepare to be boarded."

"Aye, sir."

Her long, fine hands moved on her instruments.

"Commander, *Reliant,* this is U.S.S. *Enterprise.* Surrender and stand by for boarding. I repeat: Stand by for boarding."

Lying on the deck of the bridge of *Reliant,* Khan Singh heard the triumph of the *Enterprise* communications officer. He groaned and forced himself to sit up. He would not accept defeat. Blood ran down the side of his face, and his right arm was shattered. He could see the bone protruding from his forearm. He felt the pain and accepted it, then put it aside. Shock intoxicated him and put a fine edge on his anger.

He crawled to his feet. His crushed arm flopped against his side. He picked up his useless right hand and thrust it beneath his belt, holding it steady and out of his way.

"No, Kirk," he whispered. He smiled. "Our game is not over yet. I am not quite prepared to concede."

"*Reliant,* stand by and prepare for boarding." The viewscreen was dead, but Khan did not need it to know that the *Enterprise* was approaching him, secure and arrogant in the certainty of its conquest.

Khan staggered from the bridge, toward the storage bay. . . .

Laughing.

Back on the *Enterprise,* Mr. Spock kept a close eye on his instruments and waited for a reply from *Reliant.* Perhaps Khan had been killed in the final barrage. Perhaps.

Spock did not believe it. The engines, both impulse and warp, were destroyed, and the bridge had been damaged, but he saw no evidence of a break in the hull in that area.

"*Enterprise* to *Reliant,*" Commander Uhura said again. "You are to surrender your vessel and prepare for boarding by order of Admiral James T. Kirk, Starfleet General Command."

Nothing.

"I'm sorry, sir," Uhura said. "No response."

Kirk stood up. "We'll beam aboard. Alert the transporter room."

Spock's attention was drawn to an odd energy pattern on one of his sensors. He focused and traced it: *Reliant.*

"Admiral, *Reliant* is emitting the wave form of an energy source I have never before encountered."

David Marcus, from his place near the turbo-lift, frowned and hurried to the science officer's station. He leaned over to look at Spock's sensor.

"My God in heaven," he said.

Spock raised one eyebrow.

"It's the Genesis wave!" Marcus said.

"What?"

Marcus turned toward Admiral Kirk. His face paled.

"Khan has Genesis!" David Marcus said. "He's armed it! It's building up to detonation!"

"How long—?"

"If he kept our programming . . . four minutes."

"Shit," Kirk said. He leaped up the stairs and slammed his hand against the turbo-lift controls. "We can beam aboard and stop it! Mr. Spock—"

"You can't stop it!" David cried. "Once it's started there's no turning back!"

Kirk rushed back to his place and stabbed the intercom buttons.

"Scotty!"

Kirk received no answer but static. He spoke anyway.

"Scotty, I need warp speed in three minutes or we've had it!"

The intercom crackled. No reply.

Spock watched all that occurred. He knew what Mr. Scott would say if he could even be reached: Decontamination would take at least another six minutes, and no human being would last long enough in the radiation flux even to begin the jury-rigging necessary to bring main engines on-line. He knew, from studying the Marcuses' data, the incredible velocity of the Genesis wave, and he knew the speed his ship could go under damaged impulse engines. It was no match.

"Scotty!"

Spock made a decision.

"Saavik!" Kirk said. "Get us out of here, full impulse power!"

"Aye, sir." She was prepared: at the order, the *Enterprise* spun one hundred eighty degrees in place and crawled away from *Reliant*.

Spock permitted himself a moment of pride. Saavik would make a fine officer: she would fulfill the potential he had detected in the filthy, barbarous, half-breed Hellguard child. He wished he would be able to guide her a little further.

But this way, she would be freer to find her own path.

When the doors to the turbo-lift opened, responding to Jim Kirk's abandoned order, Spock stepped inside.

Khan Singh felt hot blood flowing from his temple, from his arm, inside his body. He coughed blood and spat it out. His cold hand caressed the Genesis torpedo. It was armed and ready.

He staggered and fell to his knees.

"No," he said. "No, I will not die here. . . ."

He stumbled into the turbo-lift. It pressed upward beneath him. When it reached the bridge, he had to crawl to leave it. He collapsed finally at the top of the stairs, but he could see the viewscreen.

The *Enterprise* crept away at a painfully slow speed. Khan began to laugh. The pain caught up to him, and he coughed. He was bleeding into his lungs, into his belly. He did not have much time. But it would be enough.

"You cannot escape me, James Kirk," he murmured. "Hades has taken me, but from his heart I stab thee. . . ."

He watched the *Enterprise,* turned tail and fleeing, terrified. He laughed.

Agony took him, and he cried.

"For hate's sake . . . I spit my last breath at thee. . . ."

Joachim's body lay only an arm's length from him. His wife's body, dust, lay half a light-year distant. Soon neither space nor time would have any meaning, and he would join his love and his friend.

He crawled to Joachim, reached out, and touched his rigid hand.

Darkness enclosed his spirit.

Spock entered the engine room. Scarlet warning lights flashed through it, bloodying the forms of its crew. Dr. McCoy knelt in the middle of the main chamber, trying to save the life of an injured crew member.

The rest of the crew struggled to put more power to the impulse engines, knowing—they *must* know—that their efforts were useless. When the Genesis wave began, it would spread until it reached hard vacuum, engulfing and degrading every atom of matter within the Mutara Nebula, gas or solid, living or dead.

Without speaking or acknowledging his presence, Spock strode past Dr. McCoy to the main reactor room. He touched the override control.

"Are you out of your Vulcan mind?"

McCoy grabbed his shoulder and dragged him around by sheer force of will, for certainly the doctor's strength could not match Spock's.

Without replying, Spock looked at the doctor. He felt detached from everything: from the ship, from their peril, from the universe itself.

"No human can tolerate the radiation in there!" McCoy cried.

"But Doctor," Spock said, feeling a certain terribly un-Vulcan affection for the man who opposed him, "you yourself are fond of pointing out that I am not human."

"You can't go in there, Spock!"

Spock smiled at Dr. McCoy. He was so completely and comfortingly predictable. Spock could go through their conversation in his mind and know everything the doctor would say, everything he himself would reply. The result was the same.

"I regret there is no time for logical argument, Doctor," he said. "I have enjoyed our conversations in the past."

With that peculiarly human atavistic instinct for danger, McCoy drew back, knowing what he planned. But Spock was too quick for him. His fingers found the nerve in the junction of McCoy's neck and shoulder. He exerted pressure. McCoy's eyes rolled back, and he collapsed. Spock caught him and lowered him gently to the deck.

"You have been a worthy opponent and friend," he said.

He finished the coding for the manual override of the reactor room and stepped into the screaming radiation flux.

At first it was quite pleasant, like sunlight. Spock moved toward the reactor. The radiation increased, and his body interpreted it as heat.

He reached toward the damping rods. An aura of radiation haloed his hands; the rays spread forward, outward, even back, penetrating his body. He could see his own blood vessels, his bones. It was most fascinating.

As he worked, he recalled the events in his life that had given him intellectual, and even—he could admit it now, and who was to despise him?—emotional pleasure. Fragments of music—Respighi, Q'orn, Chalmers—and particular insights in physics and mathematics. Bits of friendship, and even love, which he never could acknowledge.

He drew the rods from their clamps; the radiation caressed him like a betraying lover.

He accepted the regrets of his life, the expectations he had never been able to fulfill: neither Vulcan nor human, he was unable to satisfy either part of his heritage. Perhaps his uniqueness compensated in some small way. He had tried to convey that possibility to Saavik, who must face and overcome the same trials.

Radiation sang in his ears, almost blocking the cries of Mr. Scott and Dr. McCoy, on the other side of the radiation-proof glass, shrieking at him to come out, come out.

"Captain, please—!" Scott screamed.

The only real captain of the Enterprise was and ever had been James Kirk. Spock had kept the ship in trust; but now it was time to return it to its true master.

Spock could feel the very cells of his body succumbing to the radiation. He wiped the perspiration from his face and left a smear of dark blood on his sleeve. Mottled hematomata spread across his hands.

Pain crept from his nerve endings to his backbone, toward his mind, and he could no longer hold it distant.

He flexed his fingers around the manual control that would bring the main engines back into use. He strained against it, and the wheel began to turn. His tortured bones and flesh opposed the control under which he held himself. He could feel his skin disintegrating against the smooth metal, which grew slick with his blood.

"Dear God, Spock, get out of there, man!" McCoy pounded on the window.

Spock smiled to himself. It was far too late.

The main engines groaned and protested, and burst back into use.

The bridge main viewscreen showed *Reliant* receding, but slowly, so slowly.

"Time!" Jim Kirk said again. It could be no more than a minute since last he had asked: they had a few seconds left and no more.

"Three minutes, thirty seconds," Saavik said.

"Distance from *Reliant.*"

"Four hundred kilometers," Chekov said.

Jim glanced at David. Meeting his gaze, his son shook his head.

"Main engines on-line!" Chekov shouted.

"Bless you, Scotty," Kirk said. "Saavik—*go!*"

She pushed the ship into warp speed without any proper preparation.

Reliant dwindled to a speck in the viewscreen.

The speck became light.

The Genesis wave hurtled toward them through the nebular dust, dissolving everything in its path. Jim watched, his hands clenched. Saavik forced one more warp factor out of the straining ship, and it plunged from the nebula into deep space.

The huge collapsed cloud began to spiral around the nexus that had been *Reliant*. It quickly coalesced, shrinking behind them. Kirk watched, awed.

"Reduce speed," he said softly.

Saavik complied. The new planet stabilized in their sight.

The turbo-lift doors opened, and Carol Marcus came onto the bridge. She did not speak.

Jim heard her, turned, reached toward her.

"Carol, my God, look at it. . . ." It was so beautiful it made him want to cry.

Carol took his hand.

Kirk opened a channel to the engine room.

"Well done, Scotty," he said.

He glanced over his shoulder at the science officer's station.

"Spock—"

He stopped, looked around the bridge, and frowned.

"Where's Spock?"

In front of him, Saavik shuddered. Her shoulders slumped. She did not face him.

"He left," she whispered. "He went . . . to the engine room." She covered her face with her hands.

Kirk stared at her, horrified.

"Jim!" McCoy's voice was harsh and intense over the intercom. "I'm in the engine room. *Get down here.* Jim—*hurry!*"

For the first time since he began his pursuit of Khan Singh, James Kirk felt cold fear.

"Saavik, take the conn!"

He sprinted for the lift.

Chapter 9

Jim Kirk pounded down the corridors of his ship. They had never seemed so long, so cold.

He caught himself against the entryway of the engine room. It was a shambles: every emergency light flashing, sirens wailing, injured crew members moaning as the medical team tended to them.

He finally managed to catch his breath.

"Spock—?"

Scott and McCoy, near the impenetrable glass panels of the reactor room, turned toward him with horror in their faces. He understood instantly what had happened, what Spock had done. Jim forced his way past them to the hatch control. Scott dragged him away.

"Ye canna do it, sir, the radiation level—"

"He'll die!"

McCoy grabbed his shoulders. "He's dead, Jim. He's already dead."

"Oh, God. . . ."

Jim pressed against the heavy glass window, shielding away reflections and light with his arms and hands.

On his hands and knees, trying to stand up, Mr. Spock hunched beside the door.

"Spock!"

Spock barely raised his head, hearing Jim's voice through the thick panel. He reached for the intercom, his hand bloody and shaking.

"Spock. . . ." Jim said softly.

"The ship . . . ?" His face was horribly burned, and

the pain in his voice made Jim want to scream with grief.

"Out of danger, out of the Genesis wave. Thanks to you, Spock."

Spock fought for breath.

"Spock, damn, oh, damn—"

"Don't grieve. The good of the many . . ."

". . . outweighs the good of the few," Kirk whispered. But found he no longer believed it; or even if he did, he did not care. Not this time.

"Or the one." Spock dragged himself to his feet, and pressed his bleeding hand against the glass.

Jim matched it with his own, as if somehow he could touch Spock's mind through the glass, take some of his pain upon himself, give his friend some of his own strength. But he could not even touch him.

"Don't . . . grieve. . . ." Spock said again. "It had to be done. I alone could do it. Therefore it was logical. . . ."

Damn your logic, Spock, Jim thought. Tears spilled down his face. He could barely see.

"I never faced *Kobayashi Maru*," Spock said. His voice was failing; he had to stop and draw in a long shuddering breath before he could continue. "I wondered what my response would be. Not . . . I fear . . . an original solution. . . ."

"Spock!"

Saavik's voice broke in over the intercom.

"Captain, the Genesis world is forming. Mr. Spock, it's so beautiful—"

Infuriated, Kirk slammed the channel closed, cutting off Saavik's voice. But Spock nodded, his eyes closed, and perhaps, just a little, he smiled.

"Jim," he said, "I have been, and will be, your friend. I am grateful for that. Live long, and prosper. . . ."

His long fingers clenched into seared claws; the agony of the assault of radiation overcame him. He fell.

"Spock!" Jim cried. He pounded the glass with his fists. "Oh, God, no . . . !"

McCoy tried to make him leave. Jim snarled and thrust him violently away. He hunched against the window, his mind crying denial and disbelief.

Much later that night, Lieutenant Saavik moved silently through the dim corridors of the *Enterprise*. She saw no one: only a few crew members remained on duty, forced to grapple with their exhaustion.

When she reached the stasis room, she paused, reluctant to enter. She drew a deep breath and went into the darkness.

Far too many of the stasis boxes radiated the faint blue glow that showed they were in operation. Protected by the stasis fields, the body of Peter Preston and the bodies of the other people who had died on this mission waited to be returned to their families.

But Captain Spock's will stated that he was not to be taken to Vulcan; his wishes would be respected.

His sealed coffin stood in the middle of the chamber. Saavik laid one hand against its sleek side. Her grief was so intense that she could react with neither rage nor tears.

In the morning, James Kirk had decreed, Spock's body would be consigned to space and to a fast-decaying orbit around the Genesis world, where it would burn in the atmosphere to ashes, to nothing.

Saavik sat cross-legged in the corner, rested her hands on her knees, and closed her eyes. She could not have explained to anyone why she was here, for her reason was irrational.

On Hellguard, if someone died at night and was not watched, their body would be gone by morning, stripped by scavengers and torn to bits by animals. Seldom was anyone buried. Saavik had never cared enough about anyone on Hellguard to remain with them through the night.

Captain Spock and Peter Preston did not need a

guard, not here on the *Enterprise*. But this gesture was the only one she could make to them, the only two people she had ever cared about in the universe.

She stayed.

She hoped Spock had heard her before he died. She had wanted him to know that Genesis worked, partly because he had respected the people who built it, so many of whom had died to protect it, but primarily because its formation meant his sacrifice had been meaningful. The creation was the result of destruction, and the *Enterprise* and all its crew would have been caught up in that instant's cataclysm had Spock failed to act as he did. Saavik had wanted Spock to know the destruction had ended, and that creation had begun.

She knew Admiral Kirk misunderstood what she had done, and why. But Saavik's essential inner core had dictated her actions then, as it did now. Admiral Kirk's opinion was of no significance.

Tears slid down Saavik's face.

Yet she remained free of the madness. Rage was absent from her sorrow. She hoped, someday, that she might understand why. Someday.

The hours passed, and Saavik let her thoughts wander. She remembered hiding, shivering and hungry, hoping to steal a piece of bread or a discarded shred of warming-fabric, outside the Vulcan exploration party's Hellguard camp. Saavik had spied on the Vulcans as they argued till dawn, with unvarying courtesy and considerable venom, about the Romulans' castoffs, particularly the half-breed children.

That was the first time Saavik had had any idea who and what she was. Only Spock had given her the potential for something more.

When, during the final battle with Khan Singh, Saavik realized Spock had left the bridge, she *knew* what he planned and what the result would be. She had been a moment away from trying to stop him.

Only the control he had taught her had kept her at her post, because it was her duty. She had regretted her action—her failure to act—ever since. In death Spock affected all those around him, just as he had in life. Someone should have taken his place whose passing no one would lament.

She might have been able to stop him: though his experience was enormously greater, Saavik was younger than he, and faster.

If she *had* been able to stop him, would she have had the courage to take his place? She wanted to believe she would have; for had she not, everyone on the ship would be dead, dissolved into sub-elementary particles and reformed into the substance of the Genesis world.

Saavik had no belief in soul or afterlife. She had read various philosophies; she accepted none. A person died; scavengers destroyed the body. That was all.

Yet as the hours passed and her concentration deepened, her feeling that somehow, somewhere, Spock's consciousness retained some of its integrity grew stronger.

"Spock," she said aloud, "can you see what has happened? Are you there? Are you anywhere? A world has formed; the Genesis wave is still resonating within the nebula, forming a new sun to give the world light and sustain its life. Soon the wave will die away, and the universe will have another star system. But it will be one among millions, one among billions, and you taught me to value uniqueness. Your uniqueness is gone."

Suddenly she opened her eyes. She thought, for a moment, she had heard something, some reply—

Saavik shook her head. The strange hours before morning could give one any mad thought.

Mr. Sulu woke slowly, coming to consciousness in the dim night illumination of sick bay. He had a raging headache, he felt as if someone were sitting on his chest, and his hands hurt. He tried to get up.

A moment later, Dr. Chapel was at his side. She made him lie down again.

"What happened?" His voice came out a hoarse croak. He tried to clear his throat. "Why—"

"The oxygen dries your throat," Dr. Chapel said. "It will go away." She held a glass so he could take a sip of water.

"We've been pretty worried about you," she said. "You're all right, though; everything's going to be all right."

He tried to touch the sore spot in the middle of his chest, but the palms of his hands were covered with pseudoskin, and he could not feel anything. He realized what the soreness must be. He frowned.

"Did I have to be resuscitated?" he asked.

Chapel nodded. "David Marcus saved your life."

"I don't remember. . . ."

"You shouldn't expect to. You were nearly electrocuted. A little memory loss is normal. Your brain scan is fine."

"What about Khan?"

"Dead." She stood up. "Go back to sleep, Hikaru."

He reached out: his hands were too stiff to stop her, but she paused.

"Chris," he said, "something more is wrong. What is it? Please."

"Mr. Spock," she said very softly.

"Spock—! What—?"

"He's dead."

"Oh, gods. . . ."

Chris Chapel started to cry. She hurried away.

Sulu stayed where he was, stunned with disbelief.

Jim Kirk sat alone in the dark of his cabin. He had not moved in hours; his mind kept turning in circles, smaller and smaller, tighter and tighter.

Someone knocked on his door.

He did not answer.

A pause. The knock again, a little louder.

"What do you *want?*" he cried. "Leave me alone!"

The door opened, and Carol stood silhouetted in the

light from the corridor outside. She came in and closed the door.

"No, Jim," she said. "I won't leave you alone. Not this time." She knelt before him and took his hands in hers.

He slumped down; his forehead rested on their clasped hands.

"Carol, I just don't . . . I keep thinking, there must be something I could have done, that I should have done—" He shuddered and caught his breath, fighting the tears.

"I know," Carol said. "Oh, Jim, I know." She put her arms around him. As Jim had held her when she grieved for her friends, she held him.

When he slipped into an exhausted, troubled sleep, she eased him down on the couch, took off his boots, and covered him with a blanket from his bed. She kissed him lightly. Then, since there was nothing else she could do for him, she did leave him alone.

When morning came, Saavik rose smoothly from her place in the corner of the stasis room. She had found a measure of serenity in her vigil, a counterweight to her grief. She bid a final farewell to her teacher and to her student, then left the stasis room. She had many duties to take care of, duties to the ship and to Mr. Spock.

The ship's company assembled, in full dress, at 0800 hours. Saavik took her place at the torpedo guidance console and programmed in the course she had selected.

Accompanied by Carol and David Marcus and Dr. McCoy, Admiral Kirk came in last.

Ths ship's veterans, the people who had known Mr. Spock best, stood together in a small group: Mr. Sulu, Commander Uhura, Dr. Chapel, Mr. Chekov, Mr. Scott. They all watched the admiral, who looked tired and drawn. He stood before the crew of the *Enterprise*, staring at the deck, not speaking.

He took a deep breath, squared his shoulders, and faced them.

"We have assembled here," he said, "in accordance with Starfleet traditions, to pay final respects to one of our own. To honor our dead . . ." He paused a long time. ". . . and to grieve for a beloved comrade who gave his life in place of ours. He did not think his sacrifice a vain or empty one, and we cannot question his choice, in these proceedings.

"He died in the shadow of a new world, a world he had hoped to see. He lived just long enough to know it had come into being."

Beside Admiral Kirk, Dr. McCoy tried to keep from breaking down, but failed. He stared straight ahead, with tears spilling down his cheeks.

"Of my friend," Admiral Kirk said, "I can only say that of all the souls I have encountered his was—" he looked from face to face around the company of old friends, new ones, strangers; he saw Dr. McCoy crying, "—the most human."

Admiral Kirk's voice faltered. He paused a moment, tried to continue, but could not go on. "Lieutenant Saavik," he said softly.

Saavik armed the torpedo guidance control with the course she had so carefully worked out, and moved forward.

"We embrace the memory of our brother, our teacher." Her words were inadequate, and she knew it. "With love, we commit his body to the depths of space."

Captain Sulu moved from the line. "Honors: *hut.*"

The ship's company saluted. Mr. Scott began to play his strange musical instrument. It filled the chamber with a plaintive wail, a dirge that was all too appropriate.

The pallbearers lifted Spock's black coffin into the launching chamber. It hummed closed, and the arming lock snapped into place.

Saavik nodded an order to the torpedo officer. He fired the missile.

With a great roar of igniting propellant, the chamber reverberated. The bagpipes stopped. Silence, eerie and complete, settled over the room. The company watched the dark torpedo streak away against the silver-blue shimmer of the new world, until the coffin shrank and vanished.

Sulu waited; then said, "Return: *hut.*"

Saavik and the rest returned to attention.

"Lieutenant," the admiral said.

"Yes, sir."

"The watch is yours," he said quietly. "Set a course for Alpha Ceti V to pick up *Reliant*'s survivors."

"Aye, sir."

"I'll be in my quarters. But unless it's an emergency . . ."

"Understood, sir."

"Dismiss the company."

He started out of the room. He saw Carol, but he could not say to her what he wanted to—not here, not now; he saw David, watching him intently. The young man took a step toward him.

Jim Kirk turned on his heel and left.

Saavik dismissed the company. She gazed one last time at the new planet.

"Lieutenant—"

She turned. David Marcus had hung back from the others, waiting for her.

"Yes, Dr. Marcus?"

"Can we stop the formality? My name's David. Can I call you Saavik?"

"If you wish."

"I wanted to tell you that I'm sorry about Mr. Spock."

"I, too," she said.

"When we talked the other day—I could tell how

216

much you cared about him. I'm sorry it sounded like I was insulting him. I didn't mean it that way. To him or to you."

"I know," she said. "I was very harsh to you, and I regret it. Starfleet has brought you only grief and tragedy. . . ."

David, too, glanced at the new planet, which his friends on Spacelab had helped to design.

"Yeah," he said softly. "I'll miss those folks—a *lot*. It was such a damned waste. . . ."

"They sacrificed themselves for your life, as Spock gave himself for us. When I took the *Kobayashi Maru* test—" she paused to see if David remembered their conversation back on Regulus I; he nodded, "—Admiral Kirk told me that the way one faces death is at least as important as how one faces life."

David looked thoughtful and glanced the way James Kirk had gone, but of course his father had long since departed.

"Do you believe, now, that he is your father?" Saavik asked.

He started. "No. Maybe. I don't know."

Saavik smiled. "We perhaps have something in common, David. Do you remember what *you* said to *him?*"

"When?"

"When you tried to kill him. You called him, if my memory serves me properly, a 'dumb bastard.'"

"I guess I did. So?"

"He is not—to my knowledge—a bastard. But I am. And if Admiral Kirk *is* your father, then I believe the terminology, in its traditional sense, fits you as well."

He stared at her for a moment, then laughed. "I'm beginning to think the 'dumb' part fits me even better."

He reached out quickly and touched her hand.

"I really want to talk to you some more," he said suddenly. "But there's something I have to do first."

"I must return to the bridge," Saavik said. "It is my watch."

"Later on—can I buy you a cup of coffee?"

"That would be difficult: one cannot buy anything on board the *Enterprise*."

"Sorry. That was kind of a joke."

"Oh," Saavik said, not understanding.

"I just meant, can we get together in a while? When you're free?"

"I would like that," Saavik said, rather surprised at her own reply and remembering what Mr. Spock had said about making her own choices.

"Great. See you soon."

He hurried down the corridor, and Saavik returned to the bridge.

The admiral closed the door of his cabin behind him and leaned against it, desperately grateful that the ceremony was over. He wondered what Spock would have thought of it all: the ritual, the speeches. . . . He would have said it was illogical, no doubt.

Jim Kirk unfastened his dress jacket, pulled it off, and pitched it angrily across the room. He dragged a bottle of brandy off the shelf and poured himself a shot. He glared at the amber liquor for a while, then shoved it away.

Too many ghosts hovered around him, and he did not want to draw them any closer by lowering his defenses with alcohol. He flung himself down on the couch. The blanket Carol had tucked around him the night before lay crumpled on the floor.

He smelled the pleasant, musty odor of old paper. He tried to ignore it, failed, and reached for the book Spock had given him. It was heavy and solid in his hands, the leather binding a little scuffed, the cut edges of the pages softly rough in his hands. Jim let it fall open. The print blurred.

He dug into his pockets for his glasses. When he finally found them, one of the lenses was shattered. Jim stared at the cracked, spidery pattern.

"Damn!" he said. "Damn—" He laid the book very carefully on the table; he laid the glasses, half-folded, on top of it.

He covered his eyes.

The door chimed. At first he did not move; then he sat up, rubbed his face with both hands, and cleared his throat.

"Yes," he said. "Come."

The door opened. David Marcus came in, and the door slid closed behind him. Jim stood up, but then he had nowhere to go.

"Look, I don't mean to intrude—" David said.

"Uh, no, that's all right, it's just that I ought to be on the bridge."

David let him pass, but before Jim got to the door his son said, "Are you running away from me?"

Jim stopped and faced David again.

"Yes," he said. "I guess I am." He gestured for him to sit. David sat on the couch, and Jim sat in the chair angled toward it. They looked at each other uncomfortably for a while.

"Would you like a drink?" Jim asked.

David glanced at the abandoned snifter of brandy on the table; Jim realized how odd it must look.

"No," David said. "But thanks, anyway."

Jim tried to think of something to say to the stranger in his sitting room.

"I'm not exactly what you expected, am I?" David said.

"I didn't *expect* anything," Jim told him ruefully.

David's grin was crooked, a little embarrassed. "That makes two of us." His grin faded. "Are you okay?"

"What do you mean?"

"Lieutenant Saavik was right. . . . You've never faced death."

"Not like this," Jim admitted reluctantly. "I never faced it—I cheated it; I played a trick and felt proud of myself for it and got rewarded for my ingenuity." He rubbed his eyes with one hand. "I know *nothing*," he said.

"You told Saavik that how we face death is at least as important as how we face life."

Jim frowned. "How do you know that?"

"She told me."

"It was just words."

"Maybe you ought to listen to them."

"I'm trying, David."

"So am I. The people who died on Spacelab were friends of mine."

"I know," Jim said. "David, I'm truly sorry."

The uncomfortable silence crept over them again. David stood up.

"I want to apologize," he said. "I misjudged you. And yesterday, when you tried to thank me—" He shrugged, embarrassed. "I'm sorry."

"No," Jim said. "You were perfectly correct. Being proud of someone is like taking some of the credit for what they do or how they act. I have no right to take any of the credit for you."

He, too, stood up, as David appeared to be leaving.

"Then maybe I shouldn't—" David stopped. Then he said, very fast, "What I really came here to say is that *I'm* proud—proud to be your son."

Jim was too startled to reply. David shrugged and strode toward the door.

"David—"

The young man swung abruptly back. "What?" he said with a harsh note in his voice.

Jim grabbed him and hugged him hard. After a moment, David returned the embrace.

Epilogue

On the bridge of the *Enterprise,* Lieutenant Saavik
checked their course and prepared for warp speed. The
viewscreen showed the Genesis world slowly shrinking
behind them. Dr. McCoy and Dr. Marcus, senior,
watched it and spoke together in low tones. Saavik
worked at concentrating hard enough not to notice
what they were saying. They were discussing the admiral, and it was quite clearly intended to be a private
conversation.

The bridge doors opened. Saavik, in the captain's
chair, glanced around. She stood up.

"Admiral on the bridge!"

"At ease," Jim Kirk said quickly. David Marcus
followed him out of the turbo-lift.

Dr. McCoy and Carol Marcus glanced at each other.
McCoy raised one eyebrow, and Carol gave him a quick
smile.

"Hello, Bones," Kirk said. "Hi, Carol. . . ." He
took her hand and squeezed it gently.

"On course to Alpha Ceti, Admiral," Saavik said.
"All is well."

"Good." He sat down. "Lieutenant, I believe you're
acquainted with my . . . my son."

"Yes, sir." She caught David's gaze. He blushed a
little; to Saavik's surprise, she did too.

"Would you show him around, please?"

"Certainly, sir." She ushered David to the upper
level of the bridge. When they reached the science

officer's station, she said to him, softly, straight-faced, "I see that you did, after all, turn out to be a bastard."

James Kirk heard her and stared at her, shocked.

"That is a . . . 'little joke,'" she said.

"A private one," David added. "And the operative word is 'dumb.'"

Saavik smiled; David laughed.

Jim Kirk smiled, too, if a bit quizzically.

McCoy leaned on the back of the captain's chair, gazing at the viewscreen.

"Will you look at that," he said. "It's incredible. Think they'll name it after you, Dr. Marcus?"

"Not if I can help it," she said. *"We'll* name it. For our friends."

Jim thought about the book Spock had given him. He was remembering a line at the end: "It is a far, far better thing that I do, than I have ever done; it is a far, far better rest that I go to, than I have ever known." He could not quite imagine Spock's questing spirit finally at rest.

Carol put her hand on his. "Jim—?"

"I was just thinking of something. . . . Something Spock tried to tell me on my birthday."

"Jim, are you okay?" McCoy asked. "How do you feel?"

"I feel . . ." He thought for a moment. The grief would be with him a long time, but there were a lot of good memories, too. "I feel young, Doctor, believe it or not. Reborn. As young as Carol's new world."

He glanced back at Lieutenant Saavik and at David.

"Set our course for the second star to the right, Lieutenant. 'The second star to the right, and straight on till morning.'"

He was ready to explain that that, too, was a little joke, but she surprised him.

"Aye, sir." Saavik sounded not the least bit per-plexed. She changed the viewscreen; it sparkled into an image of the dense starfield ahead. "Warp factor three, Helm Officer."

"Warp three, aye."

The *Enterprise* leaped toward the distant stars.

All Futura Books are available at your bookshop or newsagent, or can be ordered from the following address:
Futura Books, Cash Sales Department,
P.O. Box 11, Falmouth, Cornwall.

Please send cheque or postal order (no currency), and allow 45p for postage and packing for the first book plus 20p for the second book and 14p for each additional book ordered up to a maximum charge of £1.63 in U.K.

Customers in Eire and B.F.P.O. please allow 45p for the first book, 20p for the second book plus 14p per copy for the next 7 books, thereafter 8p per book.

Overseas customers please allow 75p for postage and packing for the first book and 21p per copy for each additional book.